THE BEATRICE

by Geoffrey Sleight

Text copyright © 2016 Geoffrey Sleight

All rights reserved

This is a work of fiction. Names, characters and events in this narrative are entirely fictitious.

THE CURSE BEGINS

OCTOBER 10th 1763

TWO SINISTER men in black hooded robes gripped the arms of a woman, dragging her towards a large wooden stake driven deep into the soil of a grassy meadow.

The breeze ruffled the woman's long black dress and swept knotted, dark hair across her sallow, sunken face as she mouthed obscenities into the air.

Roughly her captors shoved her back against the stake and tied her hands and feet behind with ropes.

Four more robed men joined them, stacking brushwood around the woman. The surrounding crowd of villagers were electrified by the scene shouting 'BURN THE WITCH!... SEND HER TO HELL!... ROAST HER ALIVE!'

The spectators pelted the staked prisoner with stones and rotten vegetables, as the hooded men piled the brushwood higher. They left for a moment, returning shortly carrying blazing pine resin torches, flickering in the shadowy twilight.

A roar of delight rose from the crowd as the men stooped with the torches to light the brushwood around the stake and its victim.

The woman continued to mouth obscenities, and some heard a terrible curse rise from her lips as the brushwood flames sprang upwards, at first licking at her bare feet, then catching on to her dress and erupting in fury.

The woman's curses turned into cries of pain and, as the heat began to fry her flesh, the cries turned to pitiful, agonising screams, the conflagration consuming all in its path to leave a mass of charcoal.

Ecstatic at the spectacle, the villagers began slowly returning to their homes as the flames gradually died away. They were relieved the witch was gone. Consigned to hell. They were safe once more.

CHAPTER 1

THE HORROR of the Beatrice Curse came to haunt me two hundred years after the witch burned at the stake.

I was a young man in the amazing days of the 1960s. A time when my world was filled with supreme confidence and belief of great things to come.

Even now, in the later years of my life, the horror of what really happened grows vivid again, as I record the terrifying events that changed everything. Events that nearly ended my life and caused me to kill. But I'm compelled to record the story, to warn a future generation.

My ambition back then was to carve out a career as an author.

Of course, the chances of succeeding were slim with so many great writers whose books exceeded my novice skills. However, I was convinced my name, Mark Roberts, would one day rate among their glorious ranks.

I'd gained good degrees in English and History at university. My father hoped I'd join the family furniture business which he'd set up as a young man in London.

But I wanted something more exciting than that. We argued. In the end he agreed he would grant me money to finance a month long stay at Deersmoor, a remote west country village in the county of Devon.

It was intended I would write my novel there and, if I succeeded in finding a top publisher, he'd happily let me follow my star. If not, I'd join the family firm.

My hope was to write in peace and tranquillity in the beautiful countryside surroundings. In reality I'd taken a step into hell.

A cab took me on the five mile journey from the train station to the village. As it travelled along the high street past the local shops, I felt I'd been transported back in time.

Everything looked so quaint. White thatched cottages and shop fronts with brown and dark green liveries declaring their businesses, butcher, baker, greengrocer and all. Nothing like the bright and colourful window displays that dazzled in west London where I lived, with the swinging 1960s bursting into life.

The cottage I rented was just a short distance from the high street, tucked along a narrow lane with a woodland opposite. It was fairly basic with a small kitchen, living room and two upstairs bedrooms, but looked ideal for providing the peace I desired.

The first week was perfect. I spent time sketching out plots for my novel and walked to the high street to pick up provisions. The world seemed as it should be.

Then came the change.

Late one afternoon I heard a loud rapping on the front door. A beautiful young woman stood there. For a second I could have been back home. She wore a cream top and dark red miniskirt with a brass buckle belt circling her slim frame. Coupled with her pixie crop chestnut hair, the style was fashionable sixties London.

She greeted me with a mixture of smile and concern.

"I'm so sorry to disturb you, but my grandmother is dying. She wants to see you," my visitor pleaded.

"Me? Why me?"

"She's heard you're a writer and wants to tell you something."

I was baffled. What could she want to tell me? A complete stranger. I agreed to come and grabbed my denim jacket.

"It's only a short walk," she said. "Just behind the high street."

As I walked beside her I introduced myself.

"I know your name," she replied. I was surprised.

"News travels fast here. No secrets," she smiled. "I'm Alison Carpenter."

She asked if I was enjoying my stay in the village and seemed puzzled that I'd want to come to this 'backwater' place, as she put it, from a city like London.

Soon we were in a street of white terraced houses and halfway down stopped at a dark blue door. Alison knocked and an older woman opened it. She peered at me suspiciously.

"This is Mark Roberts, the writer," Alison introduced us. "And this is my mother, Emma."

Her mother stepped aside to let us in. I sensed from her I wasn't welcome.

"My grandmother's in here," Alison led me to a door down the hallway. Inside an elderly woman with a drawn and colourless face, almost skeletal, stared blankly towards the ceiling from her bed.

A well dressed man in a dark suit stood nearby.

"This is Doctor Newton. He says grandmother doesn't have long to live," Alison introduced us in a whisper. The doctor nodded a greeting.

She led me to the bedside. The old woman's eyes shifted slightly to gaze at me.

"This is the writer granny," said Alison.

The old woman began to say something. I knelt down to hear her.

"Beatrice is rising again. You must stop her," she spoke in a weak, breathless voice, but the tone of concern was unmistakable. "Write about it. Tell the world. She must be stopped. I didn't start the fire."

"Who's Beatrice? What fire?" I asked.

The grandmother was exhausted. She tried to reply, but the words wouldn't come.

"That's enough," Alison's mother Emma stepped forward. "Leave her be."

Next moment the bedroom door opened.

A young woman in a red lace blouse and white mini-skirt entered, her fair hair styled in a beehive.

"I got the message to come," she sounded alarmed.

"Grandma!" She rushed to the bedside kneeling and taking hold of the dying woman's hand. Her grandmother remained motionless.

"Oh God! I think she's gone."

Alison and her mother crossed to the bed. I felt like an intruder on a deeply personal moment.

The doctor examined the old lady and announced that she'd passed away.

The women began crying. The moment was too intimate for me to remain. I whispered to the doctor I was leaving.

"It's best for now," he replied.

As I walked back to the cottage, my head was spinning with the events. The mysterious message about someone called Beatrice. That she must be stopped. And suddenly being thrust into the deathbed scene of complete strangers.

What I was meant to do to stop this Beatrice from rising made no sense. Write what about her? Stop her from doing what? Little did I know how Beatrice would become the greatest danger of my life.

Back at the cottage I settled down to writing my novel again, but the strange business at the house kept interrupting my thoughts.

An hour later came another knock at the door. I opened it. Alison had returned.

"I'm sorry about all that," she began. "I didn't mean to embarrass you. That was my sister, Barbara, who came in. I couldn't introduce you at that moment."

"It's okay. Don't worry. I thought it best to leave. Come inside."

"No, I've got to get back," Alison declined.

"I didn't understand what your grandmother was saying. She said something about stopping Beatrice rising again. I've no idea what she meant," I explained.

"Beatrice was reputed to be a witch. She was burned at the stake two hundred years ago. It's an old legend in the village," said Alison.

Now I was even more mystified.

"Don't worry about it. My grandmother was very old and her mind was wandering a lot."

With that explanation I thought all was now laid to rest.

"I came to say my gran's funeral is on Wednesday next week. We're holding a wake after the service and I thought you could come along and meet some of our friends in the village."

I was doubtful.

"I know it's not a happy occasion, but gran was ill for some time and her death was not unexpected. I'm sure she'd have been pleased to welcome you to the village."

Alison's beautiful, pleading hazel eyes captured me. I was enchanted and helpless.

"Okay. If you would like," I conceded.

"At my house, three-thirty on Wednesday." She smiled then turned and left.

Over the next few days I settled to working on my novel again. When Wednesday afternoon arrived I set off for Alison's house. I hadn't been prepared for attending a sombre occasion during my stay and could only find a black donkey jacket coupled with black jeans by way of respect.

The chatter of family and friends flowed from inside as Alison opened the front door. She wore a black dress suit and looked absolutely radiant despite the nature of the occasion. For a moment all eyes turned towards me when I entered the crowded living room, making me feel extremely self-conscious.

"So pleased you could come," said Alison. "Have some wine." She reached for a glass on a table covered with drinks and light spreads.

As I took the glass, a bearded man with curly ginger hair approached. He was dressed in a brown corduroy jacket and trousers and peered at me through dark, horn rimmed spectacles. He had the appearance of a literary or artistic person. Maybe a college lecturer.

"Is this our new resident writer?" he posed the question to Alison while staring at me.

Alison introduced us.

"Mark, meet Rupert Long. He owns our local bookshop in the high street. I'm sure you'll have a lot in common on the subject of books and authors."

We shook hands.

"Just a novice beginner," I told him modestly.

"Well, even the greats were novices once upon a time," he said encouragingly.

"So how did you get to know Alison and the family?" Rupert enquired.

Alison interrupted.

"Granny asked to see him on her deathbed. She was mumbling something about Beatrice rising again. Her mind was wandering a bit."

"Ah, Beatrice the witch. The curse." Rupert broke in. "Of course, it's the 200th anniversary of her burning at the stake in 1763."

"What's this about Beatrice?" A woman who I recognised as Alison's sister, Barbara, entered the conversation. She wore a long-sleeved black dress and her fair hair was no longer in a beehive, but spread around her shoulders. Her face was slightly harder, more businesslike than the softer features of her sister, though the woman's engaging eyes shared the same family root.

"We're just talking about grandma's last words with Mark," Alison explained.

"We haven't been properly introduced. I'm Barbara," she turned to me and shook my hand. "And this is my fiancée Malcolm Rushton."

I nodded a greeting. Malcolm was well groomed, brown short hair with a smile that looked a bit oily.

The gathering began to grow as another man joined us. A tough, sinewy face and probably in his mid-forties with a gaze that seemed to be constantly searching our every movement.

"This is police sergeant Robert Fellows, our local law and order," Alison introduced us.

"Bob please. Call me Bob. I'm not on duty now," his strict features rose to a smile.

"I hear you're a writer," the officer turned his searching gaze on me. "Not a lot happens in this village," he said.

"Only behind closed doors," Barbara joked.

The group laughed. I felt completely outside the loop among people who obviously knew each other well.

"We were talking about Alison and Barbara's grandmother," Rupert the bookshop man brought the conversation back to its earlier direction. "She told Mark about the Beatrice curse."

"I've no idea what she meant," I said.

"Well if you're interested, come to my bookshop tomorrow and I'll tell you all about it," Rupert invited me.

"What's all this about Beatrice?" The sisters' mother Emma joined us. She wore a black dress suit. Her stern face matched the darkness of her outfit.

"Rupert was telling Mark about the witch," Alison explained.

"I don't think we should be talking about all that at your grandmother's funeral reception," she said disapprovingly. "My mother was very old, muddled in her thinking. I've no idea why she should start going on about Beatrice. She was burned at the stake 200 years ago."

"Well we burn her effigy on a bonfire every year at the Burning Beatrice festival," said Alison. "Maybe in her confused state granny thought it was all real."

"She said Beatrice was rising again," I interrupted.

Emma glared at me, an unwelcome intruder on personal family affairs. Her eyes conveyed resentment at my presence. I sensed her hostility also masked an inner fear. The group fell into an embarrassed silence. I wished the floor would open up and swallow me.

"Come over here and meet some of my other friends," Alison came to the rescue and led me across to another group of people chatting.

I spent the next hour in small talk and answering questions on why I'd come to the village. Local gossip and rumours seemed to have built me into a famous author staying in their midst, instead of my true status as a rank amateur. But it felt good, if undeserved.

At the reception, I noticed a man dressed even less formally than me for the occasion in red T-shirt and blue jeans. He was strongly built and had long, straggly brown hair. His unshaven face looked permanently brooding, as if ready to attack anyone who gave him the slightest offence.

Alison noticed me occasionally glancing at him while he stood alone throughout the gathering.

"That's our cousin, Josh Williams," she answered my unspoken curiosity. "A man who keeps himself very much to himself."

As she spoke I saw him look across at us. Quickly I averted my gaze fearing he might take offence at me staring.

"He's the woodkeeper of Fellswold, two hundred acres of local woodland," Alison explained. "It borders the road across from the cottage where you're staying. Come and meet him."

I didn't particularly want an introduction, but Alison led me over to the man. I held out my hand. He grudgingly reached out and shook mine in a painful grip of iron, the sullen look on his face unchanged as if I didn't exist.

"Mark's a writer. He's staying in the village for a while," Alison attempted to lighten the air.

"I know," the man replied in a voice of disinterest. He turned and left the room.

"He doesn't say much," Alison smiled. "But he must have liked you a teeny-weeny little bit, or else he wouldn't even have shook your hand."

I was massaging my hand, which felt like it had just been removed from a metal bench clamp.

When I left the gathering, a great sense of relief came over me. Apart from Josh the woodkeeper, and the sisters' mother Emma, they were a friendly bunch. But my feeling of being an outsider remained.

Back at the cottage I wasn't in the mood for writing and made a quick ham and cheese sandwich. There was no radio or television in the cottage, so I sat on the settee in the living room drinking coffee with some lustful thoughts about Alison. I wondered if I should ask her out for a meal one night. But she probably wasn't that interested in me. Just wanting to make me feel welcome.

The memory of her grandmother came back. The woman's deathbed rambling about Beatrice the witch. And the look of fear in the eyes of Alison's mother Emma, when I recalled the dying woman's words "Beatrice is rising again."

Rupert the bookshop owner had invited me to visit him if I wanted to know more about this enigmatic Beatrice. I decided to go to his book store tomorrow.

CHAPTER 2

RUPERT was serving a customer at the counter as I entered. I waited, looking around at the bookshelves and displays. A table to one side was stacked with cut-price novels and illustrated books.

"Hello Mark," Rupert called to me as the customer left. "Welcome to my humble domain."

He came round the counter and shook my hand, looking less formal in open-necked blue denim shirt and jeans, than at our first sombre occasion meeting.

"I think I know why you're here," he smiled. "You want to know more about Beatrice, I guess."

I nodded.

"I hope yesterday wasn't a crushing bore for you," he glanced at me sympathetically.

"No. It was interesting meeting some of the locals," I replied, which was partly true.

"Come to the back office. I'll hear the bell if any customers come in." Rupert led me to a door behind the counter.

Books were stacked on shelves in his office with several piles of them resting on the floor. Papers that looked like order forms and invoices were scattered around the typewriter on his desk.

He cleared some books off another chair and invited me to sit as he settled facing me on his desk chair.

"I've heard that Vera, the late grandmother of Alison and Barbara, warned you about Beatrice the witch returning. That the family believes it was just the ramblings of an old woman."

I told him that was right.

He glanced down, as if considering his thoughts, then looked up at me with a serious gaze.

"It is, of course, possible she was just rambling." He paused again. "But I'm not so sure."

I was amazed. Was he suggesting that he thought a witch was coming back from the dead?

"Let me explain some of the story," he settled back in his chair.

"Beatrice was burned at the stake in 1763. It appears she was falsely accused of killing two children and condemned as a witch. In her dying moments burning at the stake, she issued a terrible curse of revenge and vowed to return.

"One hundred years later, a local merchant reputedly cut the throats of two children in a black magic ceremony so that he could gain immense power from her curse. Now in this anniversary year of 1963, two hundred years since Beatrice's death, I believe a ritual murder of two young children could happen again, planned by someone intending to vest themselves with black magic powers."

I was shocked, but it seemed to me like some superstitious nonsense that had survived in an old village. Rupert could see I was not entirely convinced.

"Anyway, it's some food for thought." He stood up and walked across the office, reaching for a leather bound book on one of the shelves.

"Every year the village celebrates her burning at the stake with a bonfire festival. The next one is coming up soon, and being exactly two centuries since her curse, it is a powerful time for her to rise again." He handed me the book.

"This will give you more background on local legends."

I thanked him and said I'd return it in a few days. Back at the cottage I read the book into the evening.

In a section about Beatrice, the legend ran that at one time she was a good woman who helped cure villagers with special herbs and potions.

But when a young brother and sister died under her care from a mysterious sickness, the grief stricken parents who were high ranking members of the community, accused her of being a witch and practising the dark arts.

She was arrested and committed for trial in 1763, and while in custody someone unknown slit the dead children's throats with a sword. This was given as evidence that she murdered them for a black magic ceremony. Then overnight the children's bodies disappeared. This was used as yet further evidence that Beatrice had practised witchcraft to magic them away. She was sentenced to death.

Burning at the stake, she cried out, 'I curse your village. Every hundred years that same sword will cut the throats of a young brother and sister. And I will rise to give evil power to the person who kills them.'

Her curse was soon followed by screams of agony as the flames leapt and consumed her.

The story went on to say that a local merchant, Samuel Holroyd, was believed to have used the sword to slit the throats of a young brother and sister one hundred years later in 1863, as part of a dark ceremony to raise the spirit of Beatrice. His business had been failing. Suddenly his fortunes greatly improved and he became very successful through wickedness and enslaving the will of anyone who opposed him.

Most of the villagers were farmworkers at the time, and it was said that through black magic powers he caused a poor harvest that drove many of them into poverty. The farmworkers relied on loans from him to live, and then for many years after they continued in poverty, struggling to repay his excessive interest charges. He also increased their smallholding rents.

The legend said that he eventually died a terrible death when some years later his body burst into flames through spontaneous combustion, consuming him by fire.

Much of the story appeared to me as superstitious nonsense. But Rupert saying the old lady's ramblings on her deathbed might have a semblance of truth did unsettle me. He seemed a rational man and his thought that children might be murdered, in a possible black magic ceremony on 200th anniversary of Beatrice's death, appalled me.

I wanted to find out more, and decided tomorrow I'd take the bus into Oxton, a town five miles away where I knew there was a library.

****

THE librarian led me to a room at the back of the building where reference books were generously piled on shelves all around. He was a young fair-haired man and pointed me to a section with volumes on local history.

"These will give you information about the legendary Beatrice," he said taking several books from the shelves and placing them on a nearby table. "And these have some newspaper cuttings about her," he lifted a large, leather bound volume.

"I reckon this lot will take you hours to go through, but they all contain references to Beatrice. Good luck!" The librarian smiled and left me to it. It would take me days more like, I thought, looking at the books.

There was a young man and woman, who I took to be students, engrossed in their studies at another table, but apart from that the room was empty. I began my search.

The books largely repeated legends about other local events I'd already come across in the book Rupert had given me. Moving on to the newspaper stories, it was like searching through a haystack, mostly telling of locals over the years who claimed to have seen her ghost wandering in various places at night. They all seemed to have the ring of drunken or mad delusions.

Then one story struck me like a bolt.

It was a court trial back in 1910 focussing on a woman charged with murdering her husband. Her name was Vera Langton of 7 Dalton Way in the village of Deersmoor. She was accused of killing her husband by stabbing him to death with a knife and setting fire to their cottage in order to burn his body and destroy the evidence.

Vera. The name stirred a memory. I recalled Rupert referring to the silversmith's grandmother as Vera when I was at his bookshop. She had said on her deathbed 'I didn't start the fire'.

There was no logical connection with her. I didn't know her full name. But it stuck in my mind.

The story went on to say that the woman, Vera, had made previous complaints to the police about her husband Jack's brutality to her, but these were ignored.

The prosecutor said the woman had stabbed her husband and that the steel remains of a kitchen knife had been found near his charred body.

She claimed he was drunk and had started a ritual ceremony attempting to raise the spirit of the witch Beatrice. The fire started, she said, when an oil lamp was knocked over while he was trying to attack her. She denied stabbing him and said he died because of the fire.

In the end, the newspaper article read, there was no conclusive proof Vera had killed her husband and she was found not guilty.

I had absolutely no idea if the Vera Langton in the story was Alison and Barbara's grandmother other than a sixth sense, and the fact her address at the time was in the same village of Deersmoor. Maybe Rupert could shed more light on it for me.

Next day, I really had to force myself to concentrate on my novel writing with so many questions buzzing in my head. I planned to visit Rupert that afternoon.

Mid morning there was a knock at the door. Barbara stood there looking ravishingly attractive in a short red dress, and wearing a silver necklace with a heart-shaped pendant resting between her breasts. Her fiancée, Malcolm Rushton, stood beside her.

"Can't stop long," Barbara began. "We're holding our official engagement party on Saturday at the village hall and we wondered if you'd like to come along."

I readily agreed. It sounded a happier occasion than their last family event, and might also give me an opportunity to see Alison again.

"Come in for a coffee," I invited them.

Barbara looked at Malcolm. He appeared reluctant.

"It'll be okay for a five minutes," she said to him and stepped inside. He followed.

We sat at the kitchen table where Barbara asked me how my writing was coming along. It was small talk, the weather, where they'd recently been on holiday and, more interestingly, how the villagers thought she and her fiancée were sinful because they lived together without being married.

"But we're putting that right soon, aren't we?" She looked at Malcolm. "We're tying the knot next spring."

Malcolm smiled sheepishly. He still looked an oily man to me. Good looking, but with slippery eyes, though I couldn't fault his impressive, well-tailored and obviously expensive dark grey suit. He was the picture of smartness.

As we chatted, I desperately wanted to ask Barbara if her grandmother was the Vera Langton I'd read about in the newspaper article. But I kept thinking it might cause offence if the incident was something the family preferred long forgotten.

As they finished their coffees and prepared to go, I could hold back no longer.

"Was your grandmother once involved in a murder court case?" As my question surfaced, I felt I should have phrased it less directly.

Barbara had just stood up. She stared at me in surprise. I feared I'd offended her. Malcolm was standing beside her. His non-committal manner rapidly changed to annoyance.

Silence darkened the room for a moment.

"So you've been prying into our family affairs," said Barbara, giving me an inquisitive smile which lightened the atmosphere slightly. Malcolm's expression relaxed, though his concentration on me remained guarded.

"Not deliberately," I replied, explaining I'd just been doing research on Beatrice when I happened to come across the newspaper story.

Barbara sat down again.

"Then you'll know it was all a long time ago. Her husband was a drunken fool. Thought he could raise the witch Beatrice to give him great power." She stopped for a moment gathering her thoughts.

"Grandma said he attacked her with a sword and she grabbed a knife to defend herself. In the struggle a paraffin heater was knocked over and started the fire. She escaped. He didn't."

Barbara gave a warmer smile.

"As far as I know, that's what happened."

There was nothing mentioned about a sword in the newspaper article, but since it was such a long time ago, probably nothing more would ever be known about the incident. Or so I thought at the time.

"Grandma remarried and had four children. Three of them died in childhood. Two from smallpox and the other from influenza. Only my mother, Emma, survived.

Such personal information and tragedy in the family made me feel like a dreadful intruder.

"I really didn't mean to pry," I insisted. It was true I'd come across the story unwittingly, but that didn't make me feel any better.

"It's okay," Barbara could see my turmoil. "All history now." She stood up again and I walked with them to the door.

"Don't forget the party on Saturday," Barbara leaned forward and kissed my cheek before leaving.

Now my mind really was in a spin. The guilt of feeling a family spy and the softness of that kiss. The warmth of her touch and the heady essence of her perfume gave me an erection pressing hard inside my trousers.

****

THE engagement party at the village hall was certainly a brighter atmosphere than the last time I'd met the Carpenter family and their friends.

Although the village looked generally behind the times, a DJ was playing the latest Beatles hit record, She Loves You. The dance area in the middle was filled with couples.

Barbara saw me enter.

"So glad you could come," she called loudly above the sound of the music.

As I followed her to a table laden with wine, beer and spirits, she stopped to introduce me to guests.

"We'll have to find you a partner for a dance," she said, pouring me a beer from a keg barrel. "Alison's around here somewhere. I'm sure she'd love to join you. I'll see if I can find her."

She handed me the beer and disappeared into the crowd.

For a moment I felt like a spare part. Then I heard a voice.

"Is this party hip enough for the dude from the swinging city?"

It was Rupert. He held a glass of wine.

"I was expecting ballroom dancing," I joked, as he approached.

"I hear you've been prying into family affairs," Rupert looked at me disapprovingly.

"No. I found out by accident," his remark put me on the defensive.

"It's all right, I'm not here to judge," he smiled.

"I just wanted to find more on Beatrice when I came across the newspaper article."

"Don't worry, most of the older generation in the village know all about that," Rupert reassured me.

"Though most don't think it was the entire story. I doubt we'll ever know." He took a sip of wine.

"It's rumoured the bodies of the children, murdered by the merchant in a black magic ceremony one hundred years ago, were buried in Fellswood, a local wood about half-a-mile from here. Your cottage overlooks it."

Rupert's words gave me the creeps, but I wanted to know more.

"Here she is," Barbara's voice interrupted. Alison stood beside her in yet another very sexy mini-skirt.

"No more talking. Dance!" Barbara ordered.

I wasn't sure if Alison wanted to be hoisted on me, but she took my hand and we weaved through the guests to the dance floor.

"You see. We can rock even in a backwater place like this," she said. Elvis' record Return To Sender burst into life.

Alison asked if I was enjoying my stay. I wanted to ask her if she'd go out with me on a date. A meal. A drink. My nerves held me back. Fear of rejection.

We danced and as the song was fading I finally plucked up the courage to ask. But before I could get the words out, a smartly dressed man broke in, inviting Alison to dance with him as the next record started to spin. She smiled at me and disappeared with her new partner into the crowd. I cursed myself for being so slow. So stupidly shy.

I hoped I'd get the chance to dance with her again, but she was a very popular woman, especially in that short skirt and lace top. Her invites to dance came thick and fast and then she attached herself to one particular man. They looked like more than just casual friends.

Rupert seemed to have gone and all the guests obviously knew each other well. Once again I felt like a spare part, an interloper in a different world. Shortly after I left.

For the next couple of days I tried to concentrate on my writing, but my mind wouldn't settle. Rupert telling me about the murdered children, rumoured to have been buried in the wood across the lane from my cottage, troubled me.

I hadn't been into the wood since arriving, and decided to take a walk there to refresh my my thoughts after spending the last two days mostly inside.

There was a footpath leading into the wood just a short way down the lane. It was a peaceful setting with birdsong all around. Another footpath led off through a deeper cluster of trees and the light darkened under the thicker canopy of leaves.

As I approached an opening in the wood, I caught sight of what looked like a grey stone building. The structure was derelict. Part of the roof and a side wall had collapsed. The front was crumbling and covered in ivy and lichen, but I could make out the shape of a cross carved into the stonework above the gaping arched entrance. The building appeared to be an old, abandoned chapel.

Drawing closer, I saw a wire fence erected around it with a faded 'KEEP OUT' sign on a post.

Part of the fence was broken. The building seemed in danger of collapse, but curiosity drove me to climb through the opening, carefully picking my way across the weed covered rubble to look inside.

Mostly there was more overgrown rubble scattered across the floor with ivy creeping in through the window openings and sliding up the disintegrating walls.

The atmosphere was strange, as if unseen eyes were studying me.

At the far end, the darkly discoloured wall had the lighter outline of tall cross where, I presumed, a crucifix may have once been fixed.

I edged my way across the rubble towards it and suddenly felt an intense sensation. Something, someone was staring at me from behind.

I turned.

For a second I saw two children standing at the entrance. I staggered back in surprise. Then they were gone. But the fleeting vision of their images stayed in my mind.

A boy in dark trousers, waistcoat and flat cap. A girl in a long, black dress and white mob hat.

I wasn't given to fanciful thoughts of spooks or spirits, but this was a real shock. The children looked as if they were from a past era of Victorian times. Then it struck me. The murdered children of 1863 would have been Victorians.

Feeling unsettled, I quickly worked my way across the rubble to get out of the building.

As I climbed through the fence a voice echoed loudly through the wood.

"What the hell are you doing in there?"

A figure approached. It was Josh Williams, the local woodkeeper, wearing a black waterproof coat with baggy trousers tugged into his gumboots. He held a shotgun by his side.

"That's private property and dangerous. Can't you bloody read the sign!" The man was furious.

Obviously I was in the wrong, but his rudeness annoyed me.

"You're trespassing. You should stick to the bloody footpaths," he neared, his face locked in a snarl.

"Okay. I'm sorry." I glanced at his shotgun, fearing he might use it on me if I angered him any further.

"Bloody city people coming out here and poking their noses in where it's not wanted."

He waved the shotgun.

"Clear off and don't trespass in this wood any more."

I didn't feel inclined to disobey and made my way to the footpath leading back to the cottage.

The incident left me feeling deeply upset, not least the fact that I might really have seen ghosts. How did I ever delude myself into thinking I'd find a haven of peace in this so called sleepy, remote village?

Now I definitely couldn't settle. I decided to go out that evening to a local inn called The Stag and down a pint or two of beer. Perhaps I could find some peace in a cosy setting.

A huddle of men were in close conversation at the bar as I entered the inn. This was a real old world pub with dark oak ceiling beams and a log fire burning in a large inglenook fireplace. The woman behind the bar looked familiar and after a moment I recognised her as the sisters' mother, Emma.

She remembered me and gave a muted smile, partly indicating welcome to a customer, but holding me under suspicion as a village newcomer.

"How are you?" I tried being friendly. She nodded, removing a glass from under the counter ready for me to order my drink. With such an unresponsive welcome, I felt my chance of having a relaxing pint slipping away. I asked for a glass of the local brew.

"Mark. What a nice surprise." I heard Barbara's voice from behind. "We're having a drink over in the corner. Come and join us."

My chance of having a better time suddenly increased.

I took my beer and followed Barbara over to a table where her fiancée, Malcolm, and sister Alison were sitting. My hopes were raised again as I saw the possibility of getting to know Alison better and perhaps even asking her out.

"I didn't know your mother worked here," I opened the conversation.

"It's just an evening job," Barbara replied as we sat. "Helps the landlord, whose an old family friend."

"So what have been up to. Finished your novel?" Alison asked.

"No. But I've managed to upset your cousin Josh the woodkeeper."

"How?" Barbara sounded surprised.

I told them about my walk in the wood and the unpleasant meeting with him. I didn't mention the possibility that I may have seen apparitions in the derelict chapel, in case they thought I was off my rocker.

"He's a nasty piece of work," Barbara's fiancée Malcolm joined the conversation. Until now he hadn't shown much interest at my arrival in the village.

"He does a good job as the woodkeeper, but doesn't have the first idea how to get on with people," added Alison.

She looked at me sympathetically. "Don't take any notice of him. He's like that with everyone."

"Probably best not to cross him though," Malcolm advised. "He's got a criminal record for violence. He beat up a businessman in a pub once. Accused him of trying to steal money in an investment that went wrong. Very short temper."

I could believe that.

"Now this is all a bit miserable," Barbara interrupted. "We've come out for a good time."

She turned to me.

"Are you coming to the Burning Beatrice festival in a couple of weeks time?"

I remembered Rupert telling me about the festival, but hadn't particularly thought of going.

"As well as the bonfire, there's a fair, fireworks and music," Barbara encouraged me.

It occurred this could be a great opportunity to ask Alison out.

"I don't have anyone to go with," I said, looking across at Alison.

"That's because you haven't asked," she smiled.

"Will you come to the festival with me?"

"If you'd like that," she replied.

We all laughed. My nervous fear of rejection evaporated. Nothing in the world at that moment could better my feeling of complete happiness.

We carried on chatting, mostly centred on local gossip in the village and then questions directed at me about life in London.

As we broke up to go home, I asked Alison if I could walk her back to her house. She hesitated for a moment and I realised she was planning to take a lift with Barbara and Malcolm in their mini car.

"Well okay. It's a lovely night and the short walk will do me good."

She said goodbye to her sister and we set off together.

As we walked, Alison told me she worked in the village clothes shop.

"It's all dowdy stuff they sell there," she explained. "I'd love to get a job in London selling all the latest fashions. Carnaby Street or the Kings Road. I could die for the styles they sell there."

"You look pretty up-to-date with what you wear now," I told her.

"Barbara and me have to travel thirty miles to a town that stocks the latest fashions. The modern world has by-passed this place," she said regretfully. "The village must seem very downbeat to the life you're used to. Famous people, rock bands, music everywhere."

I didn't want to tell her my life at home wasn't filled with quite the excitement she was painting, fed mostly by the media. But I felt flattered she thought I moved in such exalted circles.

We reached her house and I asked if we could meet again before the Burning Beatrice festival. A meal perhaps.

"The Wheatsheaf Inn in the village does some great food," she said. We agreed to meet there in a couple of days time.

After seeing Alison to her home, I walked back to my cottage. It was a beautiful, still night and the moon seemed almost to be smiling at me in its brilliance. At last I had a date with Alison. All was right with the world.

Back at the cottage I opened a bottle of beer to toast my success at the prospect of seeing her again. Then the phone in the living room started to ring.

It was disconnected. It couldn't possibly ring. I especially didn't want a connected phone for the purpose of peace. Perhaps the telephone exchange had reconnected it. I left the kitchen to answer the call.

"Have you come to lay us to rest?" the voice of a young boy asked. The line went dead.

For a second I thought it was some sort of practical joke. Then my blood chilled. A vision of the boy and girl I'd seen in the chapel flashed before me.

Surely not. No impossible. It couldn't possibly be. A voice from beyond?

I replaced the handset and picked it up again to check if there was any connection. It was silent. No line.

What did the voice of the young boy mean? Lay who to rest? That was weird. Spooky.

During the night I kept waking, feeling deeply unsettled, dreading the phone would ring again. Was I being haunted?

****

NEXT day the fear had subsided. There were no more calls. Somehow I managed to push the incident to the back of my mind. Perhaps I'd had a bit more to drink the previous night than I realised. It was impossible to get a call on a dead line.

But once again my concentration was blown for writing. The image of the two children in the chapel kept surfacing in my thoughts.

Was it possible I'd seen two children dressed in Victorian clothes who'd quickly run away? It seemed the only logical explanation. But why would they be dressed as Victorians? Had they been to a fancy dress party?

My curiosity was nagging me to go back. Maybe I'd see something that would reasonably explain what I'd seen. A piece of clothing that might have been dropped.

When I returned, the hole in the fence had been repaired. There was no other opening. Maybe I could break through it. But the thought of Josh the woodkeeper suddenly arriving and blasting me with the shotgun was deterrent enough. I needed to think.

Either someone was playing a trick on me or I was starting to lose my mind seeing visions and receiving calls on a disconnected telephone.

As I walked back along the footpath, wondering about my next move, something caught my eye between the trees a short distance away.

Standing beside an old oak were two children dressed in Victorian clothes like the ones I saw yesterday in the chapel. They were staring at me.

Now was my chance to catch them and find out what game they were playing. I sprung towards them, but they disappeared into thin air.

I stopped. Totally shocked. Either I was going mad, or I'd really seen *ghosts*!

It took me a few minutes to gather my wits. I was frightened, but determined to get to the bottom of it. Cautiously I walked across to where I'd seen the children, terrified they might suddenly re-appear. Ghosts were an entirely new experience to me.

The leaves around the base of the oak tree were undisturbed. No flesh and blood had stood there. What the hell was going on?

Confused, I began making my way back to the cottage. As I neared the footpath exit onto the lane, I saw two people approaching. Barbara and her fiancée, Malcolm.

"Mark!" Barbara called to me. "Getting some fresh air?"

"More like getting freaked out," I replied.

"What's the problem? Has Josh been having a go at you again?" Barbara looked concerned.

"No. I think I'm starting to imagine things." I told them about the two Victorian children I'd seen.

The couple looked at each other knowingly.

"Well," Malcolm hesitated. "There's an old rumour that two children, murdered in a black magic ritual ceremony back in 1863, were buried in this wood – and that they haunt it. But it's just an old wives tale."

"I think the trouble with you writers is having an over-active imagination," Barbara added. "You've been taking all this Beatrice stuff too seriously, and now you're starting to imagine things. Take a bit of time out to relax."

She was probably right.

"We're taking a stroll to see a friend who lives on the far side of the wood. Come with us if you like," Barbara invited me.

I declined the offer. Right now the place was giving me the creeps. We said goodbye and moved on. Then Barbara called back to me.

"I hear you've got a date with Alison tomorrow night. Just have some fun. Chill out like that a bit more."

I nodded agreement.

CHAPTER 3

I MET Alison at The Wheatsheaf. It was an old coaching inn with low beams and flagstone floors. The dining area was set at the back. Candles flickered in silver holders on the tables. The subdued lighting and log fire gave it a lovely, cosy atmosphere.

I settled for steak and chips while Alison had trout with salad.

She wore a long, red dress with a large cream bow at the front. It looked stunning on her, but I was a bit disappointed it hid her beautiful legs.

During the meal, Alison told me about some awkward customers she'd had to deal with in the clothes shop at work.

"I really need to get away from this backward village. How I'd love to get a job in London," she yearned. Her ambition was to open a fashion shop in the West End.

"I'd need a fortune to afford that though," she lamented.

The conversation gradually came round to what I'd been doing. I told her about the children I'd seen in the wood. Alison appeared puzzled. Doubtful.

"You sure you hadn't been drinking?" She made light of it, but saw I was deadly serious.

"Rupert knows all about the Beatrice legend and rumours about ghosts in the wood," she told me. "But nobody other than the old folk in the village believe it. You probably need to relax a bit more." She echoed her sister's sentiment.

The conversation soon returned to London and she asked me what life was like in the big city. It didn't seem a big deal to me since I'd lived there all my life, but to Alison it appeared to be the greatest place on the planet.

When we finished our meal I walked her home. As we said goodnight, I so much wanted to kiss her beautiful soft lips, but was torn between seeming pushy on our first date, or just taking a chance.

I took a chance. Our lips met. She didn't pull away. Those few seconds were like tasting the nectar of the gods. My heart raced. My friend below stirred rapidly for action. Slowly she pulled away.

"My mum's in and I've got an early start tomorrow."

The moment of heaven had passed.

"Can I see you again soon?" I asked. A refusal would have destroyed me.

"Meet me at The Stag pub tomorrow night. Eight o'clock."

Alison unlocked the front door and was gone.

I had no memory of returning to the cottage. The precious moment of that kiss was all I could think about.

****

THE following day I went to Rupert's bookshop. If no-one else would believe I'd seen the two Victorian children standing by an oak tree in the wood, at least Rupert would give me a hearing I decided.

He listened with great interest as I described the encounter. In his back office he took a book from a shelf and thumbed through it, stopping at a page.

"This gives details of a 1763 inquiry into the brother and sister that Beatrice was accused of killing," he told me. "There's no reference to where those children were buried and it remains a mystery likely never to be solved. I think the authorities of the day disposed of them. Probably by secretly burning them to hide their own guilt of setting up Beatrice."

He went into another room off the back office and a few minutes later returned with a bound volume of old newspaper cuttings, placing it on his desk.

"But the remains of the children who were killed by the merchant Samuel Holroyd, a hundred years later, are probably still around," Rupert spoke flipping through the cuttings.

"Fifty years ago in 1913," he stopped at a page, "a researcher looking into the murders, narrowed the possibility that the children's bodies were buried near an old oak tree a few hundred yards north-west of the chapel in the wood."

He showed me the article.

"But at the time conflict was breaking out in Europe, and people were more concerned with those events than old forgotten legends. A year later, the First World War started and everything else was on hold."

"Do you have a map of the village for 1863?" I asked.

"I've got a copy dated 1865. I can't imagine the area would have changed much in two years. It's in the back store. Hold on."

Rupert returned shortly and unrolled the map, placing it on his desk.

I studied it and saw there was no chapel indicated in the wood.

"That was built in 1893," he informed me. "It's position now is here," he pointed.

"And north-west from there?" I asked.

Rupert drew a line with his finger.

"I can't be sure. But looking at the old path routes, that could be the direction I took when I saw the children," I said. "And they were standing by an old oak tree."

Rupert gave me a doubtful, but thoughtful look.

"What are you suggesting?"

"I know it sounds mad, but I'm wondering if the spectres I saw are trying to tell me something. Perhaps that's where they're buried."

As I spoke, it sounded entirely ridiculous and I expected to be ridiculed. Ghosts can't exist my rational self was telling me.

Rupert said nothing for a moment.

"Maybe. Just maybe." He began to pace up and down.

"I don't know what you've seen. Likely just imagination after hearing all these tales. But if we were to unearth the bones of the missing children, it would be an amazing find and answer a long, unsolved mystery." Rupert seemed to be growing excited at the thought.

"Come on show me where you saw the children. We need to plan this out. It's got to be worth a try."

"What about your shop?"

"Don't worry. Not much business right now. Closing it for an hour won't hurt."

We walked to the spot in the wood where I saw the spectres. The ground around the oak had a fresh covering of falling autumn leaves.

Thankfully, Rupert's presence kept at bay the overwhelming sense of eeriness I might otherwise have felt standing in the deserted setting.

"Where did you see the children?"

I pointed to the place.

"There'll be lots of roots, but we should be able to dig through," he studied the ground.

"We can't just dig it up," I protested. "What about Josh, the woodkeeper? What if he comes along? He'll have a fit."

"Don't worry about that. I know him. And anyway, we'll come back tomorrow night and dig. I've got spades and forks. If we find nothing, no-one need ever know who dug here."

I wasn't overly convinced, but somehow I was being locked into the plan. And in truth, I was curious to know if the missing children's bodies had been buried here. At least I could put my mind to rest one way or the other, knowing whether I really had seen ghosts sending me a message, or if it was all the result of my over-active imagination.

I agreed to meet Rupert the following night at the entrance to the wood near my cottage.

That evening I met Alison at The Stag pub. To my relief her mother wasn't working behind the bar. Our date would be free from Emma's prying eyes.

We sat at a table with our drinks and I told Alison about the planned dig with Rupert in the wood. The disapproving look in her face instantly told me she didn't like the idea.

"You shouldn't go digging up old bones and bodies even if the children were buried there, which I doubt."

Her attitude made me wonder if it would be the right thing to do.

"But if they are buried there it would be an amazing find. A mystery solved," I tried to convince myself.

"And you're doing this on a whim of thinking you saw some ghosts?"

Put like that, the idea did seem a bit stupid.

"Can't do any harm," I replied, searching for a reasonable justification.

"I don't think it's a good idea to dabble in things like that. It all happened a long time ago. You should let it rest."

"Well the village celebrates the burning of Beatrice, and that was a long time ago, but no-one lets that rest." I thought I'd scored a point there.

"That's just fun. No-one takes it seriously. A night out, some music and fireworks."

I could see Alison beginning to get cross. This was not her idea of a friendly chat and an enjoyable evening. Nor mine. I didn't know it would start going down this road. I swiftly changed the subject and asked about her day.

Thankfully the atmosphere soon lightened and Alison told me how she was seriously thinking of moving to London within the next few months to find a job.

After a while the conversation came round to the imminent Burning Beatrice festival. Alison planned to dress as a witch and suggested I should come as a wizard.

"Best time of year for the shop. At least it's got some good fancy dress costumes for hire," she said, giving rare praise for the place where she worked.

Later I walked her home. A few street lamps lit the road where she lived. We said goodnight in the shadow of the canopy above her front door.

Alison started to take the door key from her bag. I placed my hands on her shoulders. She looked up and we kissed. This time not just for a brief moment. A soft, lingering kiss, our tongues searched each other. Her breasts pressed firmly on my chest. My hand moved down to caress between her legs.

The front door flew open, light spilling out. We parted in a split second. Alison's mother stood there. Glaring.

"Had a good night?" She made it sound like an interrogation.

My cheeks were burning with embarrassment. I spluttered out some words that were totally incoherent. Alison was completely calm.

"Goodnight Mark," she smiled at me. "Thank you for a lovely evening." Then she stepped inside.

Emma closed the door. Not with a slam, but not exactly quietly. I'd planned to make another date to see Alison again. Now the chance had gone. I could see her at the clothes shop. We could arrange a meet from there.

****

ALISON walked into the kitchen and made herself a hot chocolate. Her mother stood by the door.

"Are you getting serious with him?" she asked.

"Maybe. Maybe not," Alison replied, sitting down at the kitchen table.

"He's only going to be here for a short time. He'll end up getting you into trouble and then he'll be gone," Emma warned her daughter.

"Mum! I'm not stupid. This is the 1960s. There are good precautions. I don't plan to get pregnant." Alison was growing angry.

"He's a stranger. He won't want to live here with all his fanciful city ideas," Emma joined Alison at the kitchen table.

"And writing!" She uttered the words with contempt. "He'd need to get a proper job to look after you and any children."

Now Alison was angry.

"I don't plan to get married yet. Nor to get pregnant, or to have any children. I'm trying to have some fun with someone who comes from a bloody more interesting place than this dump. And I plan to get a job in a London clothes shop." Alison rounded on her mother. I want to be where things are happening!"

Alison was in full force saying things she wouldn't otherwise have said if her mother hadn't interfered.

Emma looked worried.

"When are you going to London?"

"Soon. When I'm ready." Alison snapped.

Mother and daughter were silent for a moment, both beginning to regret what they'd said.

Alison took a sip of her hot chocolate.

"They're going to dig by an oak tree in the wood, to see if they can find the bodies of the missing children murdered in 1863," Alison told her mother. "The ones who are said to have been killed in a Beatrice black magic ritual."

"Who's going to dig there?"

"Mark and Rupert. Mark says he saw the ghosts of the children in the wood."

Emma shook her head.

"I blame all this on your grandmother, telling him about Beatrice and that's she's returning again. It's all in the past. They should leave it alone. It's not wise to start interfering with the dead."

On that point Alison agreed. Not so much believing in spirits rising from the dead, but the fact this was the 1960s. She thought no sensible people would take those old superstitions seriously. It just seemed unnecessary to dig up bodies. Disrespectful.

"I hope they know what they're doing," was Emma's only other remark on the subject. She rose from the chair.

"Anyway. I'm going to bed," she kissed her daughter's head. "And you should too. You've got work tomorrow."

****

I MET Rupert the following night as agreed by the path leading into the wood. He pulled up beside me in the lane driving his black, Austin Morris Minor van.

We took a garden fork and two shovels from the back of the vehicle along with a large, power-pack torch.

Guided by the torchlight, we entered the wood. The darkness around was all consuming. Occasionally fragments of the crescent moon broke through the crowding silhouettes of the trees. The hoot of an owl echoed across the woodland. Night creatures rustled and scampered away on our approach. In the stillness our every movement was amplified, especially the twigs crackling underfoot.

We arrived at the spot by the oak. I confess to being shit scared. The thought of spectres suddenly appearing filled me with terror, as did the prospect of the woodkeeper finding us.

I wasn't sure which of the two terrified me the most. I know Rupert said he knew Josh well, but I wasn't sure if he'd ever seen the man in the violent temper I'd witnessed last time we met. If he came now, I feared I might soon be joining the ghosts.

Rupert balanced the torch on a tree root bulging from the base of the oak, tilting it so the beam lit the dig area.

The soil beneath wasn't hard to cut into after we'd scraped away a layer of leaves, but tree tap roots beneath slowed our progress.

After an hour we'd managed a depth of about three feet. Nothing found. We began to wonder if it was worth going on and rested for a moment.

"Let's just dig a bit more," Rupert encouraged me, plunging the shovel into the soil again.

I continued. Ten minutes must have passed. I threw another shovel load of soil into the growing mound beside us, now seriously beginning to lose heart.

"Stop!" Rupert cried.

I froze in terror. Was Josh approaching?

Rupert had thrown down his shovel and was beginning to examine the trench. Carefully he picked up something and held it closer to the torchlight.

It was a fob watch.

Rupert wiped away the dirt and we examined it. The timepiece was discoloured, but definitely made of silver. The watch face beneath the glass cover was entirely destroyed by black mould. Damp had seeped into it. Only the hands were still intact, but corroded.

"Someone obviously dropped it here, but why is it buried?" Rupert pondered.

"Maybe it was accidentally dropped by someone."

"Dropped by someone who buried something else here," we concluded together.

We continued digging carefully, and after a few minutes saw what looked like a bone. We scraped gently. More of the bone became visible. It began to take the appearance of a shin.

I couldn't describe what went through my head at that moment. Amazement? Triumph? Awe at unearthing a body? The bodies of the children? Had the spectres really told me where they were buried? Had we done wrong?

Rupert had no such qualms. His eyes gleamed in the torchlight.

"I think we've found them," he said, unearthing more bones.

The shape of a skeleton started coming into view. I widened the length of the trench as he abandoned the shovel and knelt down scraping the soil with his hands.

In another couple of hours we had unearthed two skeletons side by side. They looked to be little more than about three to four feet in height. They had to be the missing children of 1863.

A sense of dread now came over me. Had we unleashed some terrible curse? A portent of waiting evil gripped me.

Rupert was untouched by any such unearthly thoughts.

"This is bloody amazing," he said. "We've found them. We've solved an ages old mystery."

I raised a smile, but felt no triumph. I felt vindicated that the ghosts had been sending me a message. But I didn't think the discovery of their skeletons was entirely what they were trying to tell me.

"Right. We've got to report this to Bob Fellows, our local village policeman." Rupert stood back from the trench, the sense of excitement glowing through him.

"But it's two-thirty in the morning," I replied, glancing at my watch in the torchlight. "I can't imagine anyone's on duty at the cop shop."

"We'll go to his house." Rupert wanted no delay. "This is incredible stuff."

I was knackered and not a little troubled by our discovery. Why was *I* being targeted by the ghosts? They were murdered one hundred years ago. It seemed a long time for them to wait and pick on me. It was also two hundred years since Beatrice had been burned at the stake. Maybe she did return every hundred years.

I had an awful feeling I was being drawn into some terrible event.

****

POLICE Sergeant Robert Fellows' home was set in a small row of cottages at the end of a cul-de-sac. He opened the door wearing his pyjamas, eyes squinting from sleep. He brushed back his short, greying hair in a gesture of making himself presentable to visitors.

"We've found the skeletons of the murdered children!" Rupert announced in high excitement.

The officer stared at him as if he was a lunatic.

"The missing children from the witch ritual murder in 1863." Rupert seemed annoyed that Fellows hadn't immediately grasped the facts of something that had happened a century earlier.

"Where?" The sergeant was coming out of his slumber.

"In the wood."

"Hold on while I get dressed."

He beckoned us into the cottage's small, dimly lit hallway and disappeared upstairs. Five minutes later he was back, dressed in his police uniform. He only had a bicycle to patrol the village, so he squeezed into Rupert's van with us and we set off for the wood.

The power-pack battery for Rupert's torch was fast expiring, but there was just enough light to show the officer our find.

"You shouldn't have been digging here you know. It's against the bye-laws," Fellows enthusiasm for our discovery was less than ecstatic. "I'll have to inform county police headquarters about this. They'll probably want to question you."

We presumed he meant question us about the skeleton find and not about breaking a local bye-law prohibiting digging in the wood.

We gave him a lift back to the local cop shop so he could phone details of our find to police headquarters situated twenty miles away in Bellingham.

The sergeant got out of the van grumbling to himself. He was patently upset at being disturbed in the middle of the night.

"Now go home. I'll take this over," he told us.

We drove away to get some rest for a few hours.

Next morning there was a knock at the front door. I opened it to see Sergeant Fellows standing beside his bicycle holding the handlebars.

"A detective from police headquarters wants to see you down at the local station. Make your way down there and don't be too long about it." He mounted his bike and rode off.

I'd half expected a police car to arrive with blue lights flashing and sirens wailing. They certainly did things differently out in the sticks.

Rupert was there when I arrived at the station. He'd obviously been summoned too. We stood in the reception area where a young police officer sat behind the desk leafing through some documents.

"Don't let them know you saw ghosts," Rupert whispered to me. "They'll think you're nuts and it'll only complicate matters."

I agreed.

"We'll say we found the skeletons as a result of research I'd done, and you offered to help me with the dig. We'll just keep it plain and simple."

As he finished speaking, a side door opened and a man who looked to be in his early forties entered. Strongly built and wearing a grey suit, he directed his hard, no-nonsense gaze at us.

"Mark Roberts and Rupert Long?"

We smiled, but it wasn't returned.

"I'm Detective Inspector, George Riley. Please follow me."

We entered an interview room and sat opposite the officer.

"Now these children's skeletons you found. Why were you digging for them?"

"I'm the local bookshop owner," Rupert took the lead. "I've been doing research on a legend about a woman called Beatrice, who was accused of witchcraft and murdering two children a couple of centuries ago, though I think she was probably set up."

I wasn't sure if the detective was interested in the legend, but he listened patiently.

"While burning at the stake, she issued a curse in revenge, saying that two village children would be sacrificed in a ritual ceremony every hundred years. The ceremony would raise her from the dead and give black magic power to the murderer. It would be used to increase their wealth in a way that brought hardship to the village."

Now the detective appeared to be growing impatient.

"What's that got to do with your discovery?"

"A hundred years later in 1863, a local businessman murdered two children in a Beatrice ceremony and became wealthy, using his power to extort money and ruin the lives of many villagers. Those are the skeletons of the two children. My research worked out where they were buried."

Rupert had avoided mentioning their ghosts.

The detective scribbled some notes on the pad in front of him.

"Why did you dig there in the middle of the night? Why not daytime?" The officer was curious.

Rupert explained that digging in the wood wasn't allowed. It could take months to get official sanction, if ever.

"Don't blame my friend," he turned to me. "He's a visitor to the village. A writer. He was interested and just took up my request for help."

The detective looked doubtful, as if he wasn't being told the whole story, but didn't persist.

"Well, we can see from the condition of the bones they weren't killed and buried yesterday. But there may be further questions we need to ask you." The officer stood up.

"The victims are being removed for carbon dating and there will have to be a formal inquest that you'll probably need to attend."

He picked up his notepad.

We had the feeling the detective would rather be dealing with modern crimes, rather than being dragged from his HQ to deal with historic remains.

"For now you're free to go, but if you plan to leave the area let the local station know where you're going."

We followed the officer to reception and left.

"That wasn't so bad, was it?" said Rupert as we stepped outside.

"I'd rather have been elsewhere, but no," I replied.

We parted company and I returned to the cottage, determined to get on with my writing.

After a few hours of typing some pages, screwing them up and throwing them into the bin, I realised my mind was growing ever more distracted by the events in this blasted village. I needed some groceries and decided to take a walk to the shops.

As I strolled along the high street the headline on a billboard outside the newsagent caught my eye.

BODIES FOUND IN LOCAL WOOD

It was the front page of the Deersmoor local paper. I hurried inside and bought a copy. The story began:

'The skeletons of two children, believed to have been murdered in a legendary Beatrice witchcraft ceremony, have been discovered in Fellswold Wood by two local men.'

It went on to name Rupert and me as the ones who'd made the discovery and outlined the legend surrounding Beatrice. Suddenly I'd become a local man.

Clutching the paper, I made straight for Rupert's bookshop. As I entered he was stacking books on a shelf.

"Have you seen the local paper?" I called.

He turned, his face beaming with delight.

"Fantastic, isn't it?"

Being featured in the local paper appealed to my vanity, but I wasn't filled with the apparent joy Rupert was experiencing. He could see I wasn't on his cloud.

"Can't you see the publicity this will bring to the village. The national papers are bound to pick it up. It'll attract visitors, and that's got to be great for local trade."

The thought hadn't crossed my mind.

"And it could help your writing career. You never know, they might want to interview you about your forthcoming book."

That was a thought that appealed to me, though my book as yet wasn't exactly forthcoming.

"Books about Beatrice will probably fly off the shelves," Rupert chuckled," minus the broomsticks." He thought his pun was hilarious.

"Some of them are out of print. I'm going to see a publisher about doing some reprints."

Rupert was in a world of his own. I hoped he was right.

I wasn't sure if national newspapers would be that excited about the find of two skeletons in a backwater village, linked to a century old murder. A paragraph or two, but hardly anything to drive people here in droves.

A modern-day murder by a so called 'witch' on the other hand, would have the papers selling their grandmothers for a look-in.

But I didn't want to disillusion him. I left and went on to buy some groceries.

****

MY peace back at the cottage was soon shattered by violent, repeated banging on the front door. So much so it unnerved me. I felt under attack. I opened the door cautiously, peering out.

Josh the woodkeeper stood there. The look of fury in his face was explosive.

"What the fuck were you doing digging in my wood?" he screamed at me.

I should have just slammed the door shut, but I was transfixed in terror. He probably would have smashed the door in anyway. My eyes darted from him to the shotgun strapped over his shoulder. I tried to mouth a reply. Words wouldn't come.

"You don't know what you're meddling in, you ignorant city sod. You'll end up dead if you interfere any more."

"I was only helping Rupert. It was his idea," I managed a reply, but it sounded feeble.

This seemed to phase him for a moment.

"He should have known better and I'm going to have a word with him. Anyway, he's more likely to know what he's doing than you. Just keep out of it."

With that he stormed off. As the woodkeeper he had every right to protect the wood. But his reaction appeared well over the top. I'd end up dead if I interfered any more? Interfere in what? Was he threatening to kill me, or did he know of some impending danger?

I went to the kitchen to make a coffee, still puzzling over what he meant and beginning to wonder if I'd be better off returning to London. The busy city now appeared to offer more peace than anything round here.

Just five minutes later I heard a car pulling up on the drive outside and another rapping on the door. What now? I opened it cautiously again. Barbara's smile turned to a frown as she greeted me.

"You look worried. What's the matter?"

"I've just had a mouthful of abuse and threats from Josh," I replied, inviting her in.

"Why?"

"I don't know if you've heard, but Rupert and I have discovered what looks to be the remains of the murdered children. The ones who died in the Beatrice ritual back in 1863."

"That's why I came," Barbara's smile returned. "You're famous. I saw it in the local paper. What an amazing discovery. How did you know they were there?"

I reminded her of when I'd met her and Malcolm in the wood on their way to visit a friend. The time I told them I'd seen the children.

Barbara thought for a moment.

"Oh yes."

"You told me I was imagining things. I told Rupert about it and we dug on the spot where I'd seen them standing by an old oak tree."

"You really did see their ghosts?" Barbara was amazed. She shook her head taking it in.

At least she was interested in my story now, unlike Alison who'd more or less dismissed it.

"You must have special powers," Barbara decided. "I'd be terrified if I'd seen them."

For some reason her last words made me feel concerned, unsettled.

"Why?"

She paused for a moment as if struggling to find the right reply.

"I'd just be terrified if I'd seen ghosts."

I sensed she was reluctant to pursue the point and smiled at me again, swiftly changing the subject.

"Don't worry about Josh. He's horrible to everyone. I could believe he'd have murdered the children himself if it hadn't happened all so long ago."

We sat at the kitchen table

"Josh warned me not to interfere," I explained. "Said I could end up dead."

"That's horrible. If you interfered in what?" Barbara was curious.

"I've no idea."

"Strange man. I'd steer clear of him. Sounds like he's planning something."

Now it was my turn to change subject. I didn't want to dwell on the matter any longer.

"How's Alison?" I asked. "The other night she invited me to come to the Burning Beatrice festival dressed as a wizard."

A knowing look came over Barbara's face. She could see I was more than a little interested in her sister.

"She's going to a disco down at the local community centre tonight," Barbara informed me. "It's the only modern thing about this village. You can dance to some of the latest records."

The news made my heart sink. Alison hadn't mentioned the disco. I felt that if she was interested in me, she might have said something, invited me to come along.

"Why don't you go. Have some fun," said Barbara.

"Maybe."

"Go on," she reached out and placed her hand on my knee.

"Maybe I will, but I really ought to get on with my writing." I thought that if Alison hadn't said anything about the disco to me, I didn't want to arrive there feeling like a spare part. My pride was at stake.

Barbara smiled again and stood up.

"Well, I'd better be getting on. Just came to see someone famous in the local paper," she winked.

At the door she placed her hands on my shoulders and kissed me on the cheek, pressing her breasts on my chest.

The scent of her perfume was delicious, intoxicating. I felt my penis starting to rise. Every thought rushed from my mind other than a sudden desire to feel her body and take her there and then. She exuded sexuality and she knew it, teasing me, playing with my male weaknesses. I was on the verge of kissing her lips when she pulled away. Her eyes told me she knew what I was thinking.

"Been lovely to see you again," she said, and strolled off towards her car as I stared at her beautiful, long legs hardly covered by the shortest of short mini-skirts. Back inside I finished my coffee as the lust for Barbara began to subside.

Alison came back into my mind. She was the woman I was really developing feelings for and not just the desire for sex. It made me feel guilty lusting after Barbara. But that was stupid I reasoned. I was a free agent and Alison hadn't exactly shown she was attracted beyond me being just another guy. Why hadn't she told me about the disco? Was she going with someone else?

I decided I would go along, if only to see whether I had opposition.

CHAPTER 4

THE MUSIC grew louder as I approached the community centre, an old red-brick building set back from the high street.

Lights shone brightly through the windows. A couple were snogging by the entrance door, blissfully unaware of me edging round them to go inside.

The centre was packed. People crowding round the bar to one side and couples dancing in the middle of the hall. I looked around, but couldn't see Alison in the heaving mass. Then I heard a voice calling my name distantly through the din.

Alison waved at me from a row of tables set in a corner of the building. Dodging between dancers I made my way over.

"So you've come to the grooviest spot in Deersmoor," she joked, as I reached the table. "I thought this would be a bit down market for a boy from the swinging city." She was shouting to make her voice heard over the noise.

"Join us." Alison pointed to a chair. "We're taking a rest."

Two young woman sat either side of her, with three men opposite at the table. They were obviously paired for the evening.

"It's okay," I said, raising my hand to decline the offer. Yet again I felt like an intruder in village life.

"I'll find a friend to dance with you," Alison tried to encourage me. One of the women beside her stood up and offered.

"No, it's okay. I just heard the music and wondered what was going on," I lied.

The men with the girls turned to give me a withering look. I was distracting their pitch. I longed to know which one Alison was paired with. Until now I never knew what jealousy really felt like.

"Come on, I'll give you a dance," Alison's friend was still standing, encouraging me to take to the dance floor. One of the men at the table waved her to sit down. Her face fell, but she obeyed.

"I'll be getting on my way," I said. "Enjoy your evening."

"Don't go!" Alison called out.

I could see the men growing agitated. This was likely to end in a fight. A one to one match and I fancied my chances, but three to one and I'd likely be badly beaten up. Anyway, Alison appeared to be spoken for. I was just a visitor. A passing ship in the night. She obviously had another life and wasn't that interested in me.

I left, but felt angry. She was the woman I realised I'd fallen in love with. But it wasn't worth getting beaten up for her if she didn't want me. Just leave it alone. Stop being stupid.

I returned to the cottage feeling deeply depressed, convinced that Alison was just a local woman who would only live a local life. London's bright lights were just a fantasy for her. Yes, I was being totally pathetic. That's how dismal I felt.

Then the phone in the living room began to ring. The bloody thing was disconnected. It was them again. The children. How else could a disconnected phone ring? I didn't want to answer.

"Go away! Fucking well go away," I yelled. "I've had enough!"

The phone kept ringing, vibrating through my head like a shattering headache.

On and on, it wouldn't stop. I had to answer.

Reaching the handset I lifted it ready to slam it straight down again. But something compelled me to listen.

"You are in danger," a young girl's voice warned. Save us before it's too late!"

The line went dead.

Slowly I replaced the handset. Dazed. The world seemed to be caving in. I felt the room grow cold as if there was a strange presence watching my every move. I wanted to scream. To find some peace from this growing hell.

"What danger? Now? Soon? Was someone wanting to attack me? And how in God's name would I be able to save ghosts? From what?"

I struggled to keep a grip on my sanity. It's all a trick. The locals are playing a trick on me. Yes, that's it I reasoned and started to laugh. I was the butt of a huge practical joke. Then I feared I wasn't. I had seen ghosts. Rupert and me had found the children's skeletons on the spot in the wood where I'd seen them. That was real.

I didn't sleep well that night, waking frequently thinking I'd heard a strange sound. Footsteps. Voices. Doors creaking open. Weird images in that half world of drifting, restless dreams.

****

I WAS in the middle of eating my cornflakes next morning when I heard a knock at the door. It was Rupert.

"Sergeant Bob Fellows called in at my shop. He wants us to go to the police station for ten o'clock."

I invited Rupert in for coffee.

"It's about the skeletons we found," Rupert told me as we entered the kitchen. "The detective who interviewed us the other day wants to see us again."

We chatted, wondering what questions the officer might have in store for us now and whether we might face some action for digging without authority in the woods. I told Rupert about my unpleasant doorstep encounter with Josh the woodkeeper.

"I shouldn't worry about it," Rupert assured me. "I've spoken to him and he seems to have calmed down."

I hoped Rupert was right. We finished our coffees and left for the police station.

The stern face of Detective Inspector, George Riley, greeted us again and we were led to the same interview room, sitting opposite each other as before.

"Now carbon dating on the skeletons you unearthed puts them at around the mid 1850s to early 1860s," he reported, referring to some documents on the desk in front of him.

"Some research we've done does indicate two children went missing from this village in 1863."

"Supposedly murdered by the merchant, Samuel Holroyd," Rupert interrupted.

The detective looked at him.

"There's nothing in the records to suggest who was responsible," the detective replied. "And anyway, we don't concern our investigations with uncorroborated rumours and legends." He paused for a moment to look at us searchingly.

"On examination, the forensics noted the right thigh bones on both victims were missing." He paused again, looking at us more seriously.

"Did either of you remove them?"

We shook our heads.

"We found a fob watch," I said.

"Yes, that's accounted for," the detective confirmed.

"Maybe the thigh bones were removed by the murderer," Rupert suggested.

"No," the inspector referred to the documents in front of him." Definitely says they were broken off recently."

"Perhaps it happened when they were in transit," I offered the possibility.

"Perhaps," the officer replied. "But it definitely wasn't either of you two?"

We shook our heads again.

Leafing through the documents, Inspector Riley told us the children had received injuries to their cervical vertebrae, otherwise know as the neck bone. It appeared their throats had been viciously severed with a heavy, sharp instrument. Probably a sword.

"That fits in with the accounts of the time," Rupert interrupted again. The detective was not interested in myths and legends.

"The rest of it is a lot of technical detail. What I've told you sums up how they were probably killed."

"Have forensics been able to establish anything about the fob watch?" asked Rupert.

"It was in very poor condition, but they could see an engraving on the back of 'SH. Deersmoor'."

"SH!" Rupert sounded excited. "That could be for Samuel Holroyd, the merchant believed to have murdered the children. He must have dropped it while burying them."

"Possibly," said the detective. "Unfortunately, he's not around to interview now. No-one is ever likely to know for certain who killed them."

Inspector Riley gathered his documents together and stood up.

"You're free to go. But as I've said, you'll likely be recalled for the official inquest. Just a formality."

For the first time he smiled as we said goodbye at the station exit.

"Strange that the right thigh bones of the children's skeletons are missing," I said as we returned to Rupert's van. I was puzzled. It had been far too dark and shadowy in the woods that night to identify if all the bone parts were present.

"The forensic team may have taken samples for research," Rupert suggested," and it wasn't recorded in the report."

"Would seem odd for them to just break off two thigh bones. That would hardly be professional," I reasoned.

We got into the van and Rupert started the engine. Then he paused before pulling away. It looked as if something had just occurred to him.

"The sword used to cut the poor children's throats is still out there, buried somewhere. It carries an evil curse. It would be terrible if it came into the wrong hands. Especially this bicentenary year of Beatrice's burning."

I asked him what he meant

"I'm not sure, but someone knows where that sword is hidden and I'm more convinced than ever something awful will happen soon, connected to Beatrice's curse."

He revved the engine and pulled away.

I had a feeling too that something terrible was coming, and was seriously wondering if I should remain in this village much longer. For some reason I had an uncanny sense the event was closing in on me.

Rupert dropped me off in the high street where my first stop was to buy some fresh food.

Half-an-hour later, loaded with provisions, I was about to return to the cottage when Rupert called to me from his bookshop across the street.

As I entered he held up a copy of a newspaper.

"We've made it into the nationals. The Daily Herald."

He opened the paper and pointed to a small story at the bottom of the page headed:

'CHILD BODIES IN WOODLAND GRAVE'

It referred to us as two local men out walking with a dog that started to dig where the bones were buried, arousing our suspicions.

Where on earth they got that nonsense from amazed me.

In a few more paragraphs the article said a local witch was blamed for their deaths and hanged in 1865.

So the paper had also got the date wrong, said Beatrice was hanged instead of burned, and missed out that it was a local merchant reputed to have killed the children in 1863, one hundred years after Beatrice's demise.

Rupert seemed unphased by the fact it was a very small article and totally lacking in accuracy.

"That'll drive people to the village," he enthused. "Sales will begin to rocket."

I didn't want to burst his bubble. A few visitors in the vicinity might be interested, but once again I hardly thought the nation would flock to Deersmoor. I left him to his wishful euphoria.

While in the high street, I thought about popping into the clothes shop where Alison worked. But no. If she wasn't interested in me, I didn't want to look like a pathetic, lovelorn poodle. That was it. Move on.

****

I MANAGED to write a bit more of my novel during the rest of the day, though increasingly felt real life in this village was becoming a greater drama than my fictional ideas.

That evening, I'd just finished a snack meal when a car drew up outside followed shortly by a knock at the door.

It was Barbara.

"Sorry to disturb you again," she began. "I just want a quick word."

Inviting her inside we went into the living room. She sat on a sofa and I settled on the armchair opposite.

"I don't want to worry you," she paused. Now I was worried. What now?

"It's just something you told me." She paused again. "About seeing the murdered children's ghosts."

"Yes?" I was impatient for her to get on with it.

"Well, there's an old village legend that anyone who sees them will soon die."

Her words shocked me for a moment. Then reason took over.

"I'm sure there are all sorts of old wives tales about them," I replied confidently. "I can't go around in terror of folk tales and myths."

"No, you're right," Barbara agreed. "It's just when you told me, I couldn't help feeling concerned. It's been on my mind." She smiled that beautiful smile. "Living in a small village like this, your head gets filled with local superstitions and nonsense until you actually begin to believe it."

"Don't worry. I'll take care of myself," I assured her, though I did feel a little unsettled in the light of my weird experiences to date.

"Do you have any wine?" Barbara asked, changing the subject.

"I've got a bottle in the kitchen. Wait here and I'll get some."

Returning with a glass of wine for each of us, I drew up a small table to place them on.

"It's just white plonk ordinaire," I made the excuse for my cheapskate purchase. It felt good to have some company in my otherwise lonely turret.

Barbara asked how my novel was coming along. I replied non-committally as my attention was being drawn to more basic thoughts.

Her perfume seemed to have a hypnotic effect on me, and as we talked, she shifted now and then on the sofa, gradually revealing more of her delicious thighs in an already revealing black mini-skirt.

At one point, saying she was feeling a bit warm, she undid the top button of her white lace blouse.

Meanwhile, I was beginning to feel hot in the region of my groin, my old friend once again starting to stir for some action.

As we continued talking, she sat further back on the sofa and her legs slightly parted to give me sight of her black panties, teasingly covering that juicy opening I now longed to stroke and enter. My friend below was becoming an impatient terrier pulling at the leash.

Barbara was soon to be married. I fought to keep my instincts at bay. And what if I did attempt anything? If she wasn't deliberately urging me on, I'd end up with her storming out and my reputation ruined with the locals. Then her legs parted a little further. Inside I was growing frantic. This *was* a come on – or was it?

"Can I have another glass of wine," Barbara's request broke through my innermost thoughts. A welcome distraction, but I swear I could read mischief in her eyes.

In the kitchen I started pouring more wine.

Next moment I felt arms reaching around my waist from behind. Lips softly kissed the back of my neck. That heady perfume. Barbara pressed her body on my back, her breasts teasing me. I turned and our lips met. I caressed her body and my hand slid down under her dress and inside her tights to stroke her firming pussy. Her panties were damp with juice, enticing me to slip my hand inside. My finger searched her, rotating, caressing. Barbara gasped, urging me to keep on stroking her magic spot.

"Yes, oh yes!" she cried, her mouth wide open, her eyes glazed in heavenly pleasure.

I couldn't hold off much longer.

She drew away and quickly removed her blouse and bra. Her breasts and nipples firm and begging to be kissed. I couldn't resist. She groaned with yet more pleasure, then turned and bent forward, resting her hands on the kitchen table.

"Go on. Take me, you bastard!" she cried.

I lifted her dress, quickly removing her tights and panties, then I swiftly stripped off. All the time she was desperately urging me on.

Barbara's delicious opening arched towards me. She looked back.

"For God's sake, take me, take me!"

Bulging at breakpoint, I slid inside her. Barbara yelled and started riding frantically on my shaft, sucking me further inside, giving shrieks of unbelievable ecstasy. I reached for her breasts, stroking them as we rode to climax, shaking, groaning, panting, every thought in the world except fucking thrown away.

For a while I remained inside her as our passion slowly subsided, enjoying a fleeting moment of our bodies being as one.

When we parted, a cloud of guilt descended on me. I'd had sex with a woman pledged to another man. We dressed and I finished pouring the wine.

"That was fantastic," said Barbara. "We must do it again." She seemed to have no qualms of guilt. I wasn't against the idea though.

I handed her the glass.

"What about your fiancée, Malcolm?" I asked.

"I'm not sure," she replied, taking a sip. "I'm not sure I want to be married yet."

We returned to the living room settling on the sofa together.

"I was wondering if I could stay the night," Barbara asked.

"What about Malcolm?"

"He's away on business until tomorrow."

"I don't want to get in the way."

"You won't. Anyway, I'm not *married* yet."

She must have seen from my look I was troubled about getting involved any further.

"Don't worry. But if you're bothered I'll go."

I didn't want her to go. I was enjoying her company.

"Oh, it's Alison. You're feeling guilty about being unfaithful to her," Barbara gave me a wry smile.

"I don't think I have much future with Alison," I replied, the thought made me feel sad.

"She likes you. Don't give up. But for now we're free agents, aren't we?"

I came from a city that was meant to be the most swinging place in the world. But right now I thought Barbara had the edge on it. And it was true. I was a free agent.

She leaned across and kissed me on the cheek. Soon our lips met. We stripped off again and she straddled me on the sofa. Then we went upstairs to my bedroom and spent half the rest of the night screwing and resting, screwing and resting.

When I awoke, sunlight gleamed through the closed curtains. Barbara wasn't in the bed. The clock on my bedside table had been toppled during our night of insatiable fury. I reached for it on the floor. The hands pointed to just after nine o'clock.

Going downstairs I called to her. Silence. Looking out the window kitchen window, I saw her car was gone.

I felt exhausted. Never had I experienced a night like it. I'd had one sexual encounter before in a very brief relationship. But Barbara was extraordinary. I never knew I had such energy for it.

My worry was that her fiancée would find out. I hoped she wouldn't accidentally give anything away. Returning to bed, I slept for another hour.

After resting, and feeling the need to freshen up before concentrating on writing again, I decided to take a walk to the village.

While there I called in on Rupert. He appeared a bit downhearted. The newspaper article hadn't sparked a torrent of visitors arriving. I consoled him saying it would probably take a while for the news to filter through, even though I thought it unlikely to happen.

I left to buy some fresh milk and then started to make my way back to the cottage. A familiar voice called to me from behind. It was Alison. She was standing outside her clothes shop. I turned and walked back.

I couldn't look her fully in the eyes knowing I'd spent the previous night shagging with her sister. But she didn't seem to notice my burden of guilt. She was keen to speak to me.

"Come inside. I want to explain something to you."

It sounded intriguing.

"It's all right, the owner Mrs Collins is out," Alison held the door open for me as I entered.

"Come into the back room."

I followed.

The room doubled-up partly as an office with a desk, typewriter and shelves containing ledgers on one side, and on the other rows of clothes hanging from rails.

Alison pointed to a chair while she perched herself on the edge of the office desk, her legs and thighs barely covered by her skimpy dress, drawing me to yet more temptation.

"I'm sorry if I didn't seem very sociable at the disco," she apologised.

"It's okay, don't worry," I dismissed her concern as if it really hadn't bothered me.

"You came at a difficult time. I was working up to telling my boyfriend, Davy, that I didn't want to go out with him anymore."

"Was he the one who kept giving me dirty looks?" One of the men in the party particularly looked as though he'd liked to have punched me.

"I don't know. Might be. Anyway, I just wanted you to know I wasn't deliberately trying to give you the brush-off."

Her words filled me with joy. Maybe I had another chance with her.

"Did you tell him?"

Alison looked sad.

"I did. After the disco. I think I've broken his heart. He pleaded with me and cried. God, I can't tell you how that cut me up."

She paused.

"But we really didn't have much in common. We didn't really see eye to eye on things."

I almost had sympathy for Davy, but in truth was more selfishly interested by the fact Alison could still be mine.

"It must have been difficult for you breaking it off," I genuinely felt for her, knowing that telling someone goodbye was a deeply emotional step.

I wasn't sure if it was the right moment to seize the opportunity, but I didn't want to let it slip from me again. I had to ask.

"Would you like to come out for a meal or drink again sometime?"

Alison looked at me, then cast her eyes downwards, as if struggling to find words. After what seemed endless hesitation she replied in a regretful tone.

"My mother has warned me off you," she looked troubled.

I was not surprised, but puzzled as to why.

"She's very suspicious of strangers and wonders why you're so interested in the child murders. She says I shouldn't get mixed up in it. Especially as it's the bicentenary anniversary of Beatrice's burning."

Now I was intrigued. What did Alison's mother know? What did she fear?

"It's a small village. All sorts of silly superstitions fly around." Alison was trying to make light of it.

"Some of them may have substance," I replied. "I've seen the children's ghosts, recovered their bones, received strange phone calls from child voices on a disconnected telephone line. And I'm growing bloody terrified of this place."

Alison was silent again for a moment.

"My mother's heard about it. That's why she's worried."

"Worried about what? I wish someone would tell me."

"I honestly don't know. My mother tells me nothing. Just warns me not to get mixed up with you." The frustration in Alison's voice confirmed she knew no more than me.

"Let me speak to your mother. I'm a complete innocent in this business too. I just want to know what's going on."

"I don't think she wants to see you."

"Ask her. Just ask her. Tell her I mean absolutely no harm to you or anyone. I need to know what's going on."

Alison could see I was desperate to get to the bottom of the strange events.

She looked thoughtful, considering what I'd said.

"Come to my house tonight. I'll speak to my mum. But I can't promise she'll see you."

"Fair enough." I could only hope that she'd succeed.

We stood up ready to leave the back room. I was about to ask her again if she would come out with me on a date, but the shop doorbell rang as a customer entered.

"See you tonight at my house," Alison kissed me quickly on the cheek and hurried back into the shop. I followed her out of the room. An elderly woman waited at the counter. I felt her gaze following me as I reached the door to leave, as if she was wondering what two young people hurrying out of the back might have been up to.

I didn't care. Alison had kissed me. I returned to the cottage in euphoria.

CHAPTER 5

THAT evening I called at Alison's house. She answered the door and invited me in.

"I've spoken to my mum, but she didn't seem very pleased," Alison said in a hushed voice as we stood in the hallway.

"I asked her to at least see you. She agreed, but I don't know if she'll talk to you."

I followed Alison towards a half-open doorway at the end of the hall. We entered. A small chandelier hanging from the ceiling lit the living room. A ginger tabby cat brushed past my trousers on its way out.

Prints of horses, cats and dogs adorned the walls. Ornaments were spread on shelves and inside a couple of cabinets. Then I caught sight of light, brown hair visible just above the back of a sofa. Emma was sitting there. Alison introduced me.

"Why are you nosing into village affairs?" Emma's greeting could hardly have been less welcoming. It threw me for a moment. I stood in front of her feeling like a naughty schoolboy.

She frowned at me. Her face carried a few lines of age, which didn't detract from her still being an attractive woman. But for me the look was distinctly icy.

"I've had some very strange experiences since I came to the village," I started to explain. "Seeing ghosts of children who it seems were murdered a hundred years ago. Phone calls from them on a disconnected phone, even threats to my life from the woodkeeper Josh."

Emma stared at me, but said nothing. I felt I'd hit a brick wall.

"All of it appears to link with the legend of Beatrice and some terrible event coming." I persisted in getting a reaction from her.

She remained silent.

"Your mother told me when she was dying that Beatrice was rising. I did some research at the library and read about her being accused of murdering her husband with a knife back in 1910. There was something about a black magic ritual and that the house burnt down."

Emma's icy stare changed to a troubled look. It appeared I was now getting through to her.

"I just want to know what's going on. I'm confused. Frightened for my life. I thought you might be able to help me."

"Sit down," Emma waved me to the sofa opposite. Alison joined me.

"I've no idea if anything bad will happen on the Burning Beatrice anniversary, but I can tell you what happened to my mother back in 1910. And why she was terrified Beatrice might be resurrected." Emma's tone had softened.

"Very few know the real truth and I've never told Alison. If you ever speak of it, I'll deny it."

I agreed to her terms of silence.

"My mother, then Mrs Vera Langton, was previously married to an evil drunk. He spent nearly every penny on drink and gave her a terrible life, often beating her and on some occasions breaking her bones."

Alison gasped at the revelation, obviously totally unaware of her grandmother's earlier suffering.

"In the court case my mother denied killing her husband with a knife." Emma closed her eyes for a moment as a painful memory told by her mother rose to the surface.

"In truth she did kill him with a knife. But she had every good reason to do so." She opened her eyes and now they were filled with angry passion.

"Her husband came home one night, drunk as usual. Only this time he was holding a sword. My mother asked him why he had the weapon? Where did he get it from? He began swinging it around the living room as if attacking an invisible enemy. She feared for a her life."

Alison stared in wide-eyed amazement as the bizarre story unfolded.

"He told my mother he'd won it in a gambling debt. That it had magical power. Of course, she dismissed it as drunken talk and walked back to the kitchen where she was preparing a meal. A few minutes later he came into the kitchen. He was clutching a rooster by the neck, which he'd taken from the back garden where they kept poultry. He grabbed my mother and hauled her into the living room."

Emma paused. The memory was obviously harrowing.

"He released her and picked up the sword from the table. He told her it had witch Beatrice's magical power and had been used to slay two children. He said 'if I mix the blood of two children by cutting their throats and calling the witch, I'll become wealthy. No more money worries. Power beyond my wildest dreams.'"

Emma leaned forward as if she suddenly felt faint. Alison rose to comfort her mother, placing a hand on her shoulder. Emma looked up and raised a smile to reassure her daughter. Alison settled beside me again as her mother continued.

"Vera, my mother, was used to his odd drunken behaviour, but now she was growing concerned. He ordered her to bring a bowl from the kitchen. When she returned he informed her his next actions would be a dress rehearsal. That he planned to kidnap two children and cut their throats, but for now he would practise on the cockerel. The poor creature was struggling to escape as he continued holding it by the throat. He ordered my mother to hold out the bowl, then he cut the creature's head off with a blow from the sword. As blood spurted out, he directed it into the bowl."

Emma and Alison shook their heads in disgust. The description sickened me.

"Then he started calling on Beatrice to rise and give him power. My mother cried 'you're fucking mad'. She threw the bowl away, the blood spattering across the floor. He turned the sword towards her. He was going to kill her. She ran into the kitchen and grabbed a carving knife to protect herself. He followed her, then backed away as she pointed the knife at him, retreating to the living room."

"Are you all right, Mum?" Alison stood up. Her mother was pale, but she waved her daughter to sit down and continued her story.

"In the stand-off her husband laughed. He knew the sword's reach could easily strike her first. He swung the weapon wildly at her. The house was lit by oil lamps back then and it struck one of them on a shelf, smashing on to the floor. He was distracted by it for a second and my mother sprang forward, thrusting the carving knife into his chest. He staggered back, collapsing, the sword flying out of his hand and smashing into another oil lamp perched on the floor beside a wooden wall beam."

Emma clenched her fists in agitation.

"The oil spill from the lamp set flames rapidly spreading up the beam. Fire from the other smashed lamp was now burning into the wooden floorboards. The flames started spreading like wildfire. The curtains were soon blazing. My mother dropped the knife and ran into the kitchen to get a bucket of water. When she returned the living room was totally ablaze. She dropped the bucket. Staring in horror. Not at the fire, but at distorted faces grinning, twisting, curling in the licking flames. They were laughing evilly, calling to her. She was convinced the witch Beatrice had been summoned from the depths of hell. She ran from the cottage in terror as it burned to the ground behind her."

Emma's fingers were now nervously intertwining as she recounted the horrific experience her mother had suffered.

"Until the day she died, my mother swore the only thing stopping Beatrice returning to the flesh at that moment was the fact it was a cockerel sacrifice instead of human blood, and not the centenary year of her curse."

Alison was stunned by the story. It shocked me too.

"And that's why I don't want you meddling in the affair," Emma warned me. "If you feel you have to, I don't want you involving members of my family. There are forces of evil way beyond your understanding."

"That's terrible what happened to grandma, but don't you think it's all a bit far fetched? People don't really rise from the dead."

Alison was finding the supernatural element hard to believe. And so would I if not for the fact I'd experienced some very bizarre events.

"Heed my warning girl!" Emma stared at her daughter. Alison said nothing and the room fell silent. A question puzzled me and I had to ask.

"It said in your mother's trial they found the knife, but did they find the sword?"

Emma stared at me, a look of discomfort in her eyes. After a long silence she replied.

"My mother grabbed hold of the sword when she fled from the house and buried it in the wood. I've no idea where. She wanted it never to be found again."

"But I'm sure I've seen a...." Alison began.

"Shut up child!" her mother interrupted.

Alison obeyed.

It seemed strange, but I let it pass. I detected this was my moment to leave, not wanting to be the reason for any further family upset.

I walked back to the cottage. Emma's detailed story weighed on my mind. How her mother, Vera, must have suffered. Especially seeing Beatrice's face in the flames. Perhaps her imagination may have conjured up the images.

But what really puzzled me was the sword used in the ceremony to cut the cockerel's throat. Emma said it had been buried. Alison interrupted as if she knew something. Emma stopped her from speaking.

Why? Was there a secret?

Back at the cottage I decided on an early night. Maybe I'd see things more clearly in the morning. I was making a cup of tea to take upstairs when the phone started to ring. I ignored it, hoping the ringing would stop. It didn't. Five minutes passed and the ringing continued.

A mixture of anger and fear was rising in me. It could only be the ghost children. The bloody line was disconnected. I took my tea upstairs and placed it on the bedside table. The ringing must eventually stop. It didn't. I went downstairs again to the living room, lifted the receiver and immediately replaced it. The plan worked. Silence. I turned to leave and the phone began ringing again.

Now I was angry. I ripped the line from its socket on the wall skirting board. The phone continued to ring.

"For God's sake go away! Leave me alone!" I shouted into the receiver. For a moment there was silence.

"You must save our souls and your own life," a boy's voice pleaded. "You must destroy the witch. She is coming for us."

I slammed down the receiver as my blood chilled. The child from beyond warning me my life was in danger. I had no idea where to confront the peril. Were the villagers playing some huge practical joke on me? I wished that was the case, but feared some horror really was approaching.

Again my instinct was to just flee and go back home. But Alison. I didn't want my fear to rob me of her. Perhaps I could persuade her to come to London with me. Totally confused, I picked up the phone with its trailing line, opened the front door and threw it into a hedge bordering the driveway. At least I could get some peace without it ringing anywhere near me again. Though the chance of a restful night inside my head was extremely unlikely.

CHAPTER 6

I STUMBLED about in the morning, exhausted from weird dreams. The sound of whispering voices, fading each time I sprang awake in the night, terrified that the witch Beatrice was standing beside me.

Daylight gradually drove out the nightmare gremlins, but my head ached. I was adamant that these distractions would not stop me from writing. Settling at the living room table, it wasn't long before another interruption pulled up on the driveway.

I opened the front door to see Barbara's fiancée, Malcolm, standing there.

"I was just passing and wondered if I could have a word with you for a minute." His tone seemed a bit cryptic. I invited him into the living room, indicating an armchair for him to sit down.

"No, I can't stop long." He stared at me with a less than friendly gaze.

"A neighbour told me he saw Barbara's car parked outside your cottage the other night."

I began to fear where the point was leading and didn't like it.

"Yes. She called round on a social visit. Just wondered how I was getting on," I replied truthfully.

"But I understand she was here all night," Malcolm probed further.

"Yes," I replied, feeling myself inwardly beginning to falter. "Her car wouldn't start." Now I was into lying territory.

"So she stayed here overnight?"

"She slept upstairs in my bed and I slept down here on the sofa." My lies were now taking root.

His eyes flickered.

"It must have been an electrical fault. Damp in the carburettor or something. It started fine in the morning." I was beginning to flounder for a plausible excuse as the man whose fiancée I'd been shagging stood before me.

"That's funny," he replied, "because Barbara told me the car had run out of petrol as she arrived here, and you walked into the village to get some in a can for her next morning."

"Well that's right. I noticed the car was out of petrol so I went into the village."

Malcolm's lips curled into a smile as his eyes narrowed with suspicion. He remained silent for a moment staring at me.

"That's okay then. Just wondered." He took a step to leave, then stopped to face me again.

"I love Barbara very much. I think I'd kill anyone who stole her from me."

His warning was obvious. Any reassurance from me that I had no intention of stealing her would sound empty. My words wouldn't allay his suspicions. I said nothing. He left.

I seemed to be ever more unwanted in this village, though Malcolm had more reason to wish me gone than most. His threat to kill me was incentive enough to avoid any further intimacy with Barbara, however tempting. And she wasn't the target of my real desire.

Once again I couldn't settle to writing and decided to walk into the village to buy some fresh milk. Having no fridge, the milk was forever curdling.

Rupert saw me from the window of his bookshop and beckoned me to come inside.

"I called one of the national newspapers and explained more about the Beatrice legend and our finding the children's bones after you saw their ghosts," he sounded excited.

"The reporter seemed interested, especially the ghosts and the bit about the slaying with a black magic sword."

It sounded sick to me that children being executed with a sword would be a draw. Ghosts, fair enough, but the grisly murder of innocents? Even if it was a century ago. Grisly sold newspapers though.

"The reporter said if I could get hold of the sword, they would use library photos of some Victorian children and take pictures of the woodland spot where we found the skeletons. Work up a feature." Rupert almost tripped over his words in enthusiasm. "It would be terrific publicity for the village."

Since the press hadn't arrived in droves already, he'd obviously planned a new tactic.

"Well if that's what you want," I replied, wondering why he thought I'd be excited about it. At that moment I wanted to forget the whole business, including the history of that cursed sword. It was driving me insane.

"There's one problem," said Rupert. "I've no idea where I can find the sword." He looked at me expectantly, as if I could provide the answer. He read my puzzled frown.

"Alison," he said.

"Alison what?"

"I know that Alison's grandmother buried the sword so that no-one could ever use it again." Rupert was well versed in the Beatrice legend.

"Well then how would I know where it's buried, or Alison for that matter?"

"Alison's mother, Emma. I have a feeling she may know."

Rupert's assumption took me back to my meeting with Emma. She'd said her mother had buried the sword in the wood. Alison interrupted, as if she knew something different about it. Emma suddenly stopped her from saying anything further. Why? Perhaps Alison did know more about the sword.

"You and Alison seem to get on well together. I was wondering if you could ask her to try and get more information from her mother?"

I didn't like the idea of Rupert using me in this way.

"Whatever the family knows it's their personal business," I said. "It all happened a long time ago. Can't anyone in this village let it go?"

Rupert's face fell. He looked almost tearful. We were standing in the middle of his shop. He walked over to the counter opening the pages of a ledger.

"These are my accounts," he told me. "Do you want to see?"

I declined.

"I'm almost broke. Near bankruptcy. I desperately need some good business. Publicity could turn my fortunes around. New customers."

I felt sorry for him, but pressured to help.

"I can't promise anything," I replied, which was absolutely true. "But I'll speak to Alison."

Rupert's expression brightened.

"Yes, if you could ask. I'd be eternally grateful."

That sounded a bit over the top, and I wasn't convinced I'd succeed.

Leaving Rupert, I decided to call in at Alison's clothes shop where she was just finishing serving a customer. Alison smiled at me as the customer left.

"I hope I didn't upset your mother the other night." I approached the counter as she tidied away a couple of scarves into a drawer.

"It's okay, she's very superstitious. This Beatrice thing bothers her." Alison came round the counter. "She's worried something terrible is going to happen at the anniversary bonfire festival that's coming soon."

"I'm beginning to wonder if she's right with all the weird things happening to me," I replied, telling her about a strange phone call I had yet again from the children.

"Are you sure you're not letting your imagination run away with you?" Alison looked concerned, but didn't know what to make of it. She really did doubt the possibility of the supernatural, or that anything to fear was approaching.

"The festival will be fun, don't worry." She attempted to cheer me up.

"Which reminds me. You need a fitting for your wizard costume. It's quiet right now and my manager, Mrs Collins, is away for a few hours. I'll shut the shop for ten minutes." Alison turned the card on the door to 'Closed' and locked up, then led me by the arm into the back room.

She selected a costume from one of the rails stacked with clothes and told me to put it on in a curtained cubicle at the side of the room. I changed and came out wearing a flowing navy gown, covered in embroidered silver crescents and stars.

Alison had changed into a costume of sorts, consisting of a black top, mini-skirt and tights. The pointed hat on her head was the only item of clothing representing the image of a traditional witch. I wasn't complaining. She looked absolutely gorgeous and sexy.

"Now Mr Wizard," she waved her arm towards me as if casting a spell. "I have you in my magical power. What are you going to do about it?"

"I am your servant great witch. Do with me as you will," I laughed.

Alison approached and placed her arms around my shoulders. She was irresistible. We kissed, softly at first and then more passionately as our juices began to fire. I caressed her breasts. She sighed. I moved my hand downwards across her stomach, lifting her mini-dress and slipping my hand inside her tights, stroking her pussy through her panties.

She started to breathe quickly, moaning. Her juices seeping through the thin layer. I caught my own breath. My cock was standing to full attention, throbbing, aching for her, I slid my hand inside her knickers, fingering her soaking cleft.

"There," she gasped as my finger rounded on her clit. She gave a loud gasp, her body writhing in pleasure. I was losing control. On the verge of coming.

Alison suddenly stopped. Drew away, frantically pulling down her tights and panties.

"Behind! Take me from behind!" she screamed at me, turning to hold on to the desk. For a second Barbara came into my mind. She liked it that way too. I floundered for a moment, tugging at the wizard robe, trying to lift the front out of the way. I had nothing on underneath and pulled it over my head.

"What are you doing?" Alison looked back impatiently. I could see her fingering herself, rising to the boil. Seeing her doing that drove me insane with lust. I slid my bulging cock inside her, riding furiously. Alison rocked and writhed, bursting into screams of intense orgasm as I shuddered and cried out filling her with every ounce of my soul.

I kissed her lovingly on the nape of her neck as our fire subsided. Too soon the pressures of life forcing their way back.

We parted and Alison quickly started putting on her work clothes.

"I've got to open the shop again." She was nearly dressed when we heard the doorbell ringing and sharp rapping on the front window. I dressed rapidly and followed Alison into the shop. A middle aged, grey-haired woman peered through the glass, a sour look on her face.

"It's Mrs Ryan. She runs the antiques shop next door," Alison whispered, crossing to open up.

"Are you all right?" Mrs Ryan asked. "I heard screaming through the wall."

"No, I'm fine," Alison answered brightly. "I thought I saw a mouse in the back room and screamed. But it's gone."

I could tell Alison was on the verge of bursting into laughter as the lie for the screams tripped off her tongue. But she controlled the urge.

Mrs Ryan caught sight of me standing by the back door. Her face now showed she was putting two and two together.

"Okay, as long as you're sure," she said in a knowing tone. "Perhaps I should tell your manager there's *vermin* on the premises." Her eyes caught mine. She turned and left.

"Interfering old cow," said Alison, closing the door and turning the shop sign to 'Open' again.

"Can I see you tonight?" I asked.

"That would nice," she smiled. Then I remembered Rupert's request about the sword. I wasn't sure how I was going to approach the subject. Alison must have seen my face drop.

"What's the matter?"

"It's nothing. Just something someone wanted me to ask you," I replied, realising this wasn't the time to do it.

"I must get on now," Alison insisted. "I'll come to your place at seven o'clock tonight. I'll borrow Barbara's car and we'll go to the Cross Keys pub. It's about ten miles away, by the sea. Somewhere a bit more private from the village idiots."

"Sound wonderful." We kissed.

"Do you think I'm a hussy?" Alison's eyes widened, searching mine.

"What? Why?"

"Because of how I behaved just now?"

"I think you're beautiful, and I want us to keep on seeing each other."

We kissed again and I left.

****

THAT evening Alison arrived in Barbara's mini-car and we set off for the Cross Keys pub. The front patio overlooked a shingle beach with the light of the moon rippling on the ocean waves. The night air felt chilly, so we opted to sit inside.

The pub was a quaint old building, with dark oak ceiling beams, bowing slightly from the strain of supporting the structure for more than two hundred years.

A group of men sat together on stalls at the bar, stopping their chatter to look at us as we entered. There were only a few other people sat at the tables.

"This place is crowded in the summer," said Alison. "Mostly locals now though."

The men at the bar were paying particular attention to Alison in her mini-skirt, a few lustful smiles passing between them.

I bought a Babycham for Alison and a beer for me from the friendly, stretched waistline landlord. We made do with two packets of crisps, since the pub didn't serve meals outside the summer season. Alison apologised to me for not remembering.

"It's okay, don't worry. I'm not that hungry," I lied, actually feeling starving. "Do you want to go somewhere else to eat?"

Alison declined. I was a bit disappointed, but didn't show it. More importantly her company was all I really needed. We found a table to sit.

"How was work?" I asked.

"That bloody Mrs Ryan from the shop next door came back later when Mrs Collins, my manager was there," Alison looked concerned as she told me. "She said we had rats in the shop, and I had to explain I'd been screaming because I saw a mouse."

"My old friend below has never been called a mouse before!" I laughed.

Alison's face rose into a smile, then she burst out laughing.

"As long as it doesn't turn out to be a rat, I don't mind what you call it!"

The men at the bar looked round, wondering what we were finding so funny.

"But seriously," Alison continued. "Mrs Ryan said she'd seen a young man standing behind me. I don't think it took my manager long to twig what had been going on."

"Did she say anything?"

"No, but she didn't have to. Her look said it all. The sooner I get out of this dump the better."

Alison asked how my writing was going. There wasn't a lot to report on that front.

"You looked a bit troubled when you left the shop this afternoon. Is there something on your mind?" Alison sipped at her drink.

"It's just something Rupert wants to know. He wondered if you might be able to help me," I explained.

"Me? What can I do to help?"

"He's wondering if your mother knows where the Beatrice sword is buried. The one your grandmother was attacked with. He believes it was used to kill the Victorian children in the 1863 black magic ceremony."

Alison stared at me, completely baffled.

"He thinks it's the same sword that was also used to cut the throats of two children a couple of centuries ago, so that Beatrice could be falsely blamed for it. The reason why she issued the curse as she burned at the stake," I reminded Alison of the story.

"I know about the story. But why would he want the sword? It all sounds weird, gruesome."

"He thinks it would generate publicity for the village with a story about Beatrice. Bring in business," I explained.

"Sounds sick to me. And I'm not sure if all this magic and legend is all a load of baloney." She made her disapproval plain.

"Between you and me, Rupert says his business is on the rocks," I lowered my voice. "He's near bankruptcy. Desperate."

Alison was silent, considering what I'd told her.

"I'd like to help him. He's a nice person. But...." She paused again.

"What I'm about to tell you is strictly between us. Yes?" She looked to me for consent. I nodded.

"The sword was never buried in the wood," Alison spoke in a hushed voice. "My grandmother hid it for years, not knowing what to do with it. Eventually it ended up in the attic of our house, years ago. And as far as I know, it's still there."

I was shocked. A weapon with so much grisly legend attached to it simply stored in the attic at Alison's house. She could see the amazement in my face.

"I didn't know about it until the other night, when you saw my mother. After you left she told me it was there, stored in an old tea chest. I haven't been in the attic since I was child, and I didn't stay long then, because it was dark and creepy, and full of spider webs."

"So can I tell Rupert where it is?"

"No! You mustn't!" Alison was adamant. "My mother swore me to secrecy. She's terrified it might be used for a terrible purpose again. You mustn't tell anyone."

I promised I wouldn't, but felt sorry I'd have to deny Rupert the answer he was seeking.

"If you'd like to see the sword, I'll show you. But we'll have to go into the attic while my mother's out. She'd never forgive me if she knew I'd told you."

To see this weapon with all its notoriety would be incredible. I agreed to Alison's terms.

"But you'll have to brush any spider webs away. I can't stand them," she added more terms to my visit.

"My mother sits on the local parish council. She'll be out tomorrow night at one of the meetings, so come round at seven-thirty and we'll go into the attic," Alison outlined the plan.

We chatted on for a while and then returned to the village. I invited her in for a goodnight drink, but she declined.

"If you get me going, I'll oversleep for work." Alison leaned across from the driver's seat and we kissed. I promised I'd be round the following night.

Inside the cottage and with Alison gone, I felt an overwhelming sense of loneliness. Images of my family entered my mind. How I missed the company of familiar faces.

After making a cup of tea, I went into the living room to sit quietly for a while. Then I saw it. My blood curdled!

The telephone I'd thrown into the hedge the other night was back on the side table, the cord dangling down beside it. How did it get there? Who put it back? I felt a cold sweat rising on my forehead. The device seemed almost alive, as if the dial was staring at me, smiling, enjoying my terror.

I stepped back, dreading it would ring again. My urge was to pick it up and throw it out of the cottage again. But what if it mysteriously returned? Perhaps I hadn't thrown it out. Perhaps I'd imagined doing that.

I slammed the living room door shut and went upstairs to the bedroom. If the damned phone did start ringing, I'd ignore it no matter how long it went on. The ensuing silence was eerie. The tense anticipation of the phone ringing now seemed worse.

Again I had troubled dreams in a shallow sleep, unable to rest, waiting and waiting for that cursed phone to ring, yet dreading it happening. That night it never came.

In the morning I reasoned that someone had obviously seen the phone in the hedge and brought it into the cottage. The owner renting the property to me probably. He'd have a key. Though what he would have made of me throwing his phone around I don't know. Of course, it seemed a far fetched assumption, but so did the thought of something supernatural returning it. I just wanted a logical explanation, and for now the human element would do.

I wrote a little more of my book during the day, but mostly kept nodding off into fitful sleep. My unsettled night was catching up.

That evening I set off for Alison's house, hoping Emma would have left for her meeting before my arrival. Alison opened the door, noticing the look of caution in my face.

"It's okay, mum's out. Come in."

With great relief I stepped inside.

I wanted to tell her about the strange event of the telephone mysteriously re-appearing, but feared she might think I was a total fruitcake. I wasn't sure Alison believed any of the supernatural encounters I'd experienced.

"We'll have to be quick, just in case my mum comes back early," she warned.

We went upstairs to the landing. Alison brought me a chair from her bedroom so I could reach up for the catch on the attic lid and release the ladder inside. She gave me a torch and I mounted the steps, hoisting myself into the inky darkness above.

The torch beam picked out an electric fire, several chairs, an old treadle sewing machine and a collection of scattered cardboard boxes. Then the light hit a tea chest in the far corner.

"I think I can see it," I called down to Alison.

"Are there lots of spiders?" she asked in a troubled voice.

The attic was filled with webs dangling everywhere. I attempted to reassure her.

"Some webs. But not too many. I'll brush them out of the way."

Alison climbed in, letting out a yell as the torch beam caught webs hanging freely between the roof beams.

"It's okay, the spiders are long dead," I said, sweeping some of them away with my hand. Reluctantly she followed me across to the tea chest, dust rising into the air with each step.

We reached the chest. A white sheet covered in dusty grime was draped over the side, but there was nothing inside the container.

"Someone must have taken it," Alison sounded alarmed. "My mother told me it was here just the other night."

"Maybe she's taken it," I suggested.

"I couldn't imagine she'd ever want to see it again," Alison was certain. "Perhaps it was removed some time ago and mum didn't know. I'm sorry I can't show it to you."

"Don't worry." I was disappointed, but there was nothing to do about it.

Then I noticed there were marks in the dust around the tea chest indicating that someone else must have been in the loft recently. Perhaps whoever took the sword.

I said nothing to Alison, not wishing to cause her alarm, but I was feeling troubled. And she was keen to get out of the dingy setting. This was not her comfort zone.

"I better not tell mum," she said, as we returned to the landing below. "She'll only worry."

"And she'll wonder why you went up there in the first place," I warned her. "I don't want her accusing me."

"My mother terrifies you, doesn't she?" Alison laughed.

"Too right."

We went downstairs to the kitchen and Alison made a pot of tea.

"The Beatrice bonfire festival is coming soon. You'll have to come to the shop that evening and I'll fit you out in the wizard costume," Alison poured our cups of tea and we sat at the kitchen table. Then we heard a key turning in the front door lock.

"God! It's my mother. She's come back early." Alison looked horrified. "Quick! Behind the door."

She scooped up my cup and dumped it in the sink out of sight as I rapidly hid behind the half-open kitchen door.

"Alison. Hello. I'm back," Emma called. She came to the door, looking in on her daughter seated at the kitchen table sipping tea.

"I left the meeting early," Emma sounded angry. "There's a new member of the council who poured scorn on my idea to have baskets of hanging flowers in the high street next summer."

Controversy over hanging baskets in the high street were of little interest to me at that moment, or any moment for that matter. I feared if Emma found me behind the door in her present mood she'd hang me instead of a basket.

"Why don't you sit down in the living room and try to relax," Alison suggested to her mother.

"I'm furious," Emma continued. "That bloody new upstart who's only been on the council five minutes!" Emma stepped further into the room. If she closed the door she'd see me. My legs were actually trembling with fear.

Alison stood up and took her mother by her arm.

"Come into the living room. I'll make you a cup of tea. It'll calm your nerves."

I remained hidden, agonising if I should make a run for it as they left.

"Quick!" Alison whispered, returning shortly. "Slip out the front door now!"

I needed no second prompting.

"Don't make a noise. I'll speak to you soon." She closed the door quietly as I made my escape.

Walking back to the cottage, the thought of the missing sword came to mind. I'd have to give Rupert the disappointing news tomorrow. And even if it had been in the loft, I couldn't have betrayed Alison's confidence.

But who would have taken it from the attic? And so near the 200th anniversary of Beatrice's burning? Something bad really was going to happen. Of that I was becoming more convinced.

Then another thought struck me. Rupert seemed to have an almost obsessive interest in the sword. Did he really want it just for publicity purposes? Or did he have another agenda? Could he have got into Alison's home and taken it? That didn't strike me as likely. But then a lot in this village didn't add up to normal.

CHAPTER 7

A REFRESHING breeze and the morning sun shining in a clear blue sky revitalised me as I made my way to Rupert's bookshop.

There was no-one about when I entered. A pile of books rested on the counter. Wondering if he'd nipped out for a moment, I decided to come back later. I turned to leave, when he emerged through the back room door, carrying more books which he added to the pile on the counter.

"Just having a tidy out," he said. "What brings you here on this beautiful, sunny morning?"

"I saw Alison last night at her house and asked about the sword," I began. Rupert stopped sorting through the books and gave me his full attention.

"Her mother says she has no idea where the sword is buried in the wood," I explained, which was true. That's what she told me.

But I had to keep my promise to Alison, and not tell him the sword had been hidden in the family attic for years and was now missing.

Rupert's gaze felt searing, almost as if he was detecting me hiding something.

"Did Alison or her mother ask why you were interested in it?" Rupert wondered.

"I just said I was interested in the history of it," now I felt uneasy starting to lie.

Rupert stared at me a little longer then began sorting through the books again.

"Ah well. Never mind."

I was puzzled by his matter of fact response, since only a short time ago he'd been desperate to know of the sword's whereabouts as a way of salvaging his business through publicity.

Did he know the sword had been taken from the loft and where it was now kept? I thought of asking him, but he was hardly likely to say. Otherwise he would have told me when I came in. Unless he had another agenda.

"Anyway. Thanks for trying." Rupert turned and disappeared into the back room. I felt embarrassed as if a bond of trust had been broken. A barrier of suspicion was growing between us.

Leaving the bookstore, I walked a short distance along the high street when Alison called to me. She stood in the doorway of her shop. I turned and walked back to her.

"My mother knows the sword is missing," she whispered in alarm.

"How? Does she know we went into the attic?"

"No. She was still angry about the meeting that she left early last night. I tried to calm her by telling her about my day at work. I said we'd had lots of fittings for the Burning Beatrice festival."

"So how did that make her know the sword is missing?" I was mystified.

"She just said 'God, the sword! I've got to check it's still there.' She went into the attic and saw it was gone."

"And?"

"She called round at our local policeman's house, Sergeant Bob Fellows, and told him it had been stolen."

"I thought the sword was a family secret. Surely she wouldn't tell the police it's still around?"

"There are a lot of strange confidences in a village like this. I imagine he knows more about local people and their secrets than anyone else. And he's a friend of my mother's."

This place was becoming more of a mystery to me daily

"Well, it's not good someone's taken it, but what has that got to do with us?"

"It's not so much us as you," Alison told me.

"Me?" I was stunned. "Why me?"

Alison raised her finger to her lips, asking me to keep my voice down. Not to make a scene.

"Other people in this village are very suspicious of strangers. My mother knows you're interested in the child murders and the legends," Alison explained. "She's got it in her head that you're up to no good. You're being here will cause trouble."

I was staggered by Alison's words. I'd come here to write a book in a peaceful setting. Now I was unwittingly the focus of some strange conspiracy. My mind was made up. I would just stay in the cottage and write my book. Or perhaps even return to London. Maybe I could persuade Alison to join me, where she could fulfil her ambition to work in a London fashion boutique. I was lost in these thoughts when Alison broke the next bit of bad news.

"I think Sergeant Fellows is going to call round at your cottage today to have a chat with you."

"What? Does he really think I took the sword? That's ridiculous."

"Of course you didn't. But my mother has a lot of influence in the village," Alison was apologetic. "I think he's going to warn you off."

Anger rose in me. What a petty, stupid place this was. It turned my feelings around. Now I felt determined to stay and finish my project, I would not be driven out by a bunch of backward fools.

I had no more to say to Alison. I headed back to the cottage without another word, determined to single-mindedly continue with my book. But my head wouldn't settle to it. Half-an-hour later there was a knock at the door.

I opened it to Sergeant Fellows.

"Can I have a few words, please?" he asked in a tone that wouldn't take a refusal.

I invited him in, but no further than the hallway. I had no desire to make him feel welcome.

His tall height and uniform had an intimidating effect.

"I think you know enough of the old stories about the child murders and the black magic rituals surrounding them in this village," he began.

I nodded.

"You and Rupert from the bookshop found the children's skeletons. You saw their ghosts, didn't you, or something like that?"

I said yes, but detected there was a hint of cynicism in his voice, as if I'd made up the story about seeing ghosts. Then it struck. Rupert and me had never told the police that I'd seen the children's spirits over their grave.

"How do you know I saw their ghosts? I've never said that to the police." I thought it would trip the officer. He was silent for a moment, unphased.

"This isn't London," he replied. "Word spreads in this place as easily as butter on bread. There are no secrets here." He paused. "Except one."

I was puzzled.

"Something evil is going to happen on the Burning Beatrice festival night this year. It's two hundred years since she was burned at the stake."

The sergeant gave me a searching look.

"Do you know anything about the missing sword?"

For a moment I was stuck for a reply. Was he trying to find out if I knew it had been hidden in the loft? Trick me? Try and accuse me of taking it? As far as everyone else knew, other than Alison, I'd only heard it was buried somewhere in the wood.

"What missing sword?" I feigned ignorance. "The Beatrice one is buried in the wood. So I've heard. If that's the one you mean."

His eyes searched me for a little longer. Then he changed the subject completely.

"So you want to be a famous writer?" he asked. I was completely thrown by his change of mood.

"Just a writer for now," I replied. "Might take a bit of time to become famous."

Sergeant Fellows laughed.

"It's a small place this village. Sometimes wish I'd had the courage to branch into bigger things. But there you are. You live with your decisions."

My attitude towards the officer started to change from caution to sociability. Perhaps I'd underestimated him as just a village plod.

"Well, I'd better be going," he said.

He stepped outside then turned back to me.

"Remember, there are lots of gossips in this place, and some will pretend to be your friend when they're not. If you think there's anyone planning something suspicious for the Beatrice festival night, let me know straightaway."

I assured him I would.

Closing the door, I was left with the impression the sergeant had received a whisper of some plan to carry out a terrible act on the festival night, and he was in the process of narrowing down possible suspects. Fortunately, it appeared that he'd taken me off the suspect list. But I still couldn't shake off the dread that I would become involved in the feared evil plot.

Now I began to feel guilty about leaving Alison so abruptly outside her shop. I wanted to tell her the good news that I hadn't been arrested, or ordered to get out of the village by the sergeant. I decided to go back and apologise.

As I neared Alison's premises in the high street, I saw the woodkeeper, Josh, coming out of Rupert's shop with a book in his hand. It surprised me. I didn't think Josh was a man of literature.

I decided to call in at Rupert's on the pretence I'd left a set of keys there earlier. Maybe I could discover in a roundabout way what book Josh was carrying. I didn't trust the man and my suspicions of both him and Rupert were growing.

Rupert helped me search round the shop, but obviously I knew we'd never find the keys because I had them in my pocket.

On leaving, I thanked him for his help and casually mentioned I'd just seen Josh coming out of the shop with a book.

"I didn't think he was a man of words," I remarked lightheartedly, hoping to coax the name of the book out of him.

Rupert smiled at me.

"There's a lot more to Josh than people give him credit for," he said enigmatically.

I smiled back, not quite sure what to make of his cryptic reply, then left.

The feeling in me grew that there was something going on between the two. But what, I had no idea. Only that it felt a bit odd.

Suddenly I began to think I was going native. My mind starting to sink to the level of an inbred villager, suspicious of every little action that didn't fit with my own prejudices.

Why shouldn't a woodkeeper be interested in books. But no matter how much I tried, I couldn't place him as a man of reading. Rude and ignorant was the only way I could describe him.

More importantly for now, I wanted to tell Alison that Sergeant Fellows had called and he didn't suspect me of stealing the sword.

She was folding clothes on the counter when I entered.

"Sergeant Fellows came round and he doesn't think I took...."

Alison placed a finger to her lips to silence me, and pointed to the door behind the counter indicating someone else was present.

"Wait outside and I'll pop out."

I left the shop and waited for a moment. Alison came out.

"My manager is doing stocktaking in the back room. I can't stop long," she said.

I told her the good news that I wasn't a suspect for taking the sword.

"I'm so glad," she smiled, "but I've got to get back. I'll call you tomorrow night. I can't get away from here 'til late because I'm helping my manager with the stock-take."

We kissed quickly and Alison returned.

She obviously bore no grudge against me for my earlier tantrum when I stormed off. That alone made me happy. I'd been worried she might have taken offence and not want to see me again.

I headed back to the cottage along the high street. Next second a shop door opened and a man hurried out colliding with me. I nearly fell over. When I looked it was woodkeeper Josh. He didn't seem to care he'd nearly knocked me down, he was stooping to pick up a book from the pavement. I caught sight of the title. *Legends of the Witch*.

"Look where you're going you clumsy sod!" he yelled at me, then walked on. I felt like shouting abuse back, but he probably could have flattened me on the spot if angered him any further.

What interested me was Josh's choice of reading. Legends about the witch. Beatrice I presumed. It must have been the book he was holding when he came out of Rupert's shop earlier. I'd wondered if the two were up to something. Now the thought was reinforced. Rupert didn't seem concerned that I couldn't tell him where the sword was hidden. Were they involved in its sudden disappearance?

I wondered if I should report my suspicions to Sergeant Fellows. But I'd told him I knew nothing about the sword. I didn't want to be drawn back into a web of suspicion again. I returned to the cottage wondering what I should do. Maybe this could lead the officer to a possible black magic link between the woodkeeper and Rupert. Or was I letting my imagination run away with me again? Something strange was going on.

Entering the cottage I saw a letter on the floor. It was from my mother. She'd written to say that my father had suffered a minor heart attack. I was shocked. She said he was now back home and in good spirits and didn't want me to make a fuss or worry about it. She asked after my health and how my writing was progressing.

I couldn't just leave it, I had to call home. Obviously the phone in the cottage was no use except, it seemed, for paranormal contact. There was a phone box in the village. I ran all the way to it, anxious to make sure my father was still recovering well.

"It's all right," my mother reassured me, "you're father is doing fine. But he's got to let others take on more of his business responsibilities."

I felt guilty that I wasn't there to help.

"I'll come back straightaway and do whatever he needs," I said.

"No, you don't have to. It'll push his blood pressure up again if he thinks he's being a burden," she replied. "There are people in the company who could and should be doing more. You do your own thing for now. There's plenty of time for life to burden you later."

I told my mother to give him my love and to telegram me quickly if I needed to come back.

Her comment about plenty of time for life to burden me later echoed through my mind. If only she knew how burdened I felt with the jigsaw this village had sprung on me. But I wasn't going to trouble her with yet more problems when I knew that under her strong facade she was likely going through hell with worry.

If I went back my father would be upset by the fuss, possibly making him worse, and that would distress her even more. Now I knew what being between a rock and hard place really meant.

Back at the cottage again I couldn't settle to writing. My efforts at being a 'writer' seemed trivial compared to everything happening around me. Instead of finding creative freedom it felt more like being imprisoned. The turmoil in my head continued as the day faded to night.

At ten o'clock I decided to go for a walk to help clear my thoughts before going to bed. The prospect of sleep seemed far away.

There was no street lighting along the lane outside the cottage so I took a torch to see the way. Reaching the footpath into the wood, I decided to stroll along it for a while. Communing with nature might help to settle me.

I'd travelled a short distance into the darkness of the woodland, the torch beam picking out tree trunks and leafy ground foliage, when I heard voices in the distance. Who else could be in the wood at this hour? It sparked my curiosity. I changed direction and left the path crossing the woodland undergrowth towards the sound.

The voices grew louder as I approached. I turned off the torchlight so I wouldn't be detected. As my eyes adjusted to the darkness, I could just make out the shapes of the tree trunks and trod carefully to keep down the sound of crackling twigs underfoot. Soon I could see a clearing ahead. As I grew closer, the jagged outline of the tumbledown chapel came into view. It appeared strangely ominous set against the starlit sky.

I bent down and moved forward slowly. Next second I tripped on something in the darkness and fell flat on my face, crying out in surprise. Then I felt an arm wrap round my forehead, pulling it back, and a hand clamping my mouth.

"Shut up or I'll kill you with my knife!" a woman's voice threatened.

I didn't want to argue.

"One sound and that's it!" the woman released her hold on me. I lifted myself and turned to see my attacker. In the darkness it took a moment to register. I recognised the shadowy highlights of the face. It was Barbara!

She stared back in disbelief.

"What the hell are you doing here?" Our amazement tumbled out together.

But the question was pushed to one side as Barbara whispered to keep quiet. The voices had stopped. We could see two figures walking from the chapel towards us. They must have heard my cry of surprise when I fell.

Barbara told me to lay flat on the ground. She did the same. The scrunching of leaves underfoot grew louder as the figures grew nearer, their torch beams sweeping the ground on the lookout for intruders.

They reached the edge of the clearing and entered the wood, moving ever closer to where we were hiding.

My heart was beating to burst. I fought to remain as quiet and still as possible. I could almost smell danger in the air.

The torch beams were almost upon us. Only the fortune of having a large tree trunk nearby saved us from detection, casting a shadow that their lights didn't strike. The footsteps stopped.

"Probably a fox attacking something," came a man's voice.

"Yes, some night creature," his companion agreed.

For a moment I couldn't believe what I was hearing. They were the voices of Josh the woodkeeper and Rupert. What were they doing at the chapel?

Both men turned and began walking back to the building. Then stopped.

"I don't think we're going to find the sword in the chapel," said Josh. "I read the book you gave me. Lots of possibles where it could be, but it could be months, even years, checking them all out."

"I could have sworn the sword was hidden somewhere in the chapel," Rupert replied.

"Well, I've had a good look round here in the past and your idea of it being in a container under the memorial stone hasn't come to anything," Josh grumbled. "I think I've put my back out trying to lift it with you tonight."

"I'm sorry," Rupert apologised. But we need to find it before the festival. Everything rests on our taking control." The two began walking again, returning to the main path out of the wood. Barbara and I remained silent until we were sure they were far away.

"What the hell are they up to?" I whispered to her, remaining cautious about being overheard.

"Good question," she replied as we stood up.

"Me and my fiancée, Malcolm, have been suspicious about those two for a while now. We think they may be hatching something terrible to happen at the Burning Beatrice festival."

Her words echoed the thoughts that had been growing in my own mind.

"At one point we thought you might be involved with them," Barbara said to my utter amazement, as we started walking back to the main path from the wood.

"Why me?"

"Because you helped Rupert to discover the children's skeletons. It looked like you were into something dark together, discovering them because you saw their ghosts."

"But I did see their ghosts!" I protested. "It wasn't anything hatched with him. He just seemed desperately keen to find the missing children and persuaded me to help."

"There you are," she replied. "It was driven by him. And now maybe he's tricking Josh into his plan."

"Do you think....?" I hesitated. "Do think he may be planning to.....do evil to some children on festival night? In a black magic ritual?" The thought was abhorrent to me.

"Who knows?" said Barbara.

Soon we reached the main footpath and decided it was safe to turn on the torch.

"Malcolm and I have been keeping tabs on Rupert and Josh for some time. I saw them in the bar where my mother works when I went in to see her a few hours ago. They were in a huddled sort of conversation, so I decided to follow them when they left," Barbara explained.

"Strange how you were in the woods tonight too," she rounded on me.

"Hold on! I was just going for a walk to clear my head. I've had a very stressful day. I heard voices and wondered who it was at this time of night." My explanation wasn't exactly one that provided conclusive proof, but it was true. I had no other.

"It's all right. I believe you," said Barbara, much to my relief.

"For a city boy coming from big swinging London, you strike me as a bit too naïve to be into any bad business," she told me frankly.

"I'm not entirely naïve though," I replied. "I know the sword is missing and that it isn't buried anywhere."

Barbara stopped in her tracks.

"How do you know it's missing?" she demanded.

"Alison told me. She was going to show me the sword. She said your grandmother hadn't buried it. That it was stored in the attic. We went up there together, but it was missing."

Barbara seemed stunned.

"Alison shouldn't be telling you these things. Who else has she opened her mouth to?" She sounded extremely concerned.

"I take it you knew it was kept in the attic?" I asked Barbara.

"Grandmother told me a few years ago, but she swore me to secrecy. I guessed my mother probably knew about it, but I never spoke of it to anyone." She paused.

"Does Alison know what's happened to it?"

I shook my head. Barbara frowned.

We continued walking and then left the woodland pathway entering the lane leading to my cottage.

"Sergeant Fellows, came round to ask if I knew about the sword," I explained. "I denied knowing anything. I didn't want to get Alison into trouble. She didn't want your mother to know we'd been looking for it in the attic."

"The only trouble is if Josh and Rupert haven't got the sword, who has?" Barbara wondered.

"Sergeant Fellows asked me to tell him if I came across anything suspicious," I told Barbara. "Maybe I should tell him what we heard tonight."

"You could do. Though he's not the sharpest tool in the box and he could hardly arrest Josh and Rupert for being in the woods late at night," she sounded doubtful. "I'm going past the police station tomorrow. I'll pop in and tell him if you like. But I can't imagine he can do anything without some strong evidence. That's what we need."

I agreed, thinking the officer was likely to take more seriously the word of a local than a city outsider. I had a feeling that Sergeant Fellows didn't quite trust me, even though he'd shown a friendly face.

We stopped at the driveway to my cottage. I assumed Barbara's car was parked nearby and she'd want to go home.

"Do you mind if I come in for a moment to freshen-up?" she asked.

I felt wary of inviting her inside. Fantastic though the lustful sex we'd had the other night had been, I was worried prying eyes might come to the wrong conclusion and report back to Malcolm. But I couldn't refuse her simple request.

"Yes, come in," I said as we left the lane and approached the front door. Turning on the light we could see dirt and leaf pieces clinging to our jeans and jackets, gathered from sprawling on woodland undergrowth. Barbara laughed as we stood in the hallway brushing off the muck as best we could with our hands.

"I need the bathroom," she said, and made her way upstairs.

I went into the living room, collapsing on to the armchair, feeling tired after all the tension.

Soon I heard Barbara coming down the stairs and entering the living room wearing only her bra and panties. To say I was gobsmacked would be a total understatement. I felt my old friend below rising and pressing hard against my flies.

"I've sponged down some of the mud on my clothes," she said, as if there was nothing unusual about her appearance. "I laid them across the clothes dryer in your spare bedroom. Give them half-an-hour and they should be fine to wear again."

I was speechless and hypnotised by seeing her in her underwear. I wanted her. But the threat her fiancée had given surfaced in my mind. I didn't want to get into yet more difficulty for what in reality would be a fleeting thrill. Alison appeared in my thoughts, making me feel guilty about my lust. The animal in me was seeing things differently though.

"How about a drink before I go?" Barbara asked, sitting on the sofa opposite, her legs spread slightly open with that beautiful, soft mound between them covered only by a thin layer of cream, lace panties.

"I can make you a tea or coffee," I heard myself stuttering, trying to maintain control.

"Haven't you anything a bit stronger? A glass of wine or a bacardi?"

"I've got a quart bottle of cider."

"Cider! Yes, that'd be nice. I haven't had cider for ages."

I went to the kitchen and took the bottle from a cupboard with a couple of glasses. My resolve to control the situation was slipping away. The thought of possessing Barbara grew stronger. I returned and poured the drink.

"Why don't you sit with me?" she invited, patting the sofa cushion beside her.

I hesitated. Then spoke frankly.

"Because I'm terrified your fiancee will find out you've been here again. He called round after you'd been here the other night and gave a veiled threat that he'd kill me if I stole you from him."

Barbara listened, Then smiled.

"He's really a pussy cat. He couldn't harm anybody. Between you and me, I told him once how Alison and me sometimes used to 'play' with each other. Sisters' secrets. And I could see he was totally turned on by it."

Barbara revealed the intimate details in such a matter of fact manner. But it had a powerful impact on me too. Whether it was true or not, the vision of the two sisters pleasuring each other came into my head. Barbara was deliberately leading me on.

I took a heavy gulp at my cider. She stood up and came to me, brushing a hand over my flies and softly stroking my intense hard-on. Then she reached behind her back unhooking her bra and letting it drop to the ground. She bent forward, pressing her lips firmly on mine and resting her bare breasts on my chest, rotating them and lustfully searching inside my mouth with her tongue.

I had no more control.

Her hand unzipped my flies and reached inside, holding my yearning shaft, ready to explode in orgasm. Then she released it.

"Not just yet, big boy," she ordered.

She guided my hand to her panties and held it to stroke her crotch as she started to sigh. I slipped my hand inside and felt her urging juices, softly stroking and sliding my finger into her delicious quim.

"Oh my God!" she cried, rubbing pleasurably. "Get your bloody clothes off and fuck me!"

I literally tore off my clothes.

"Get on the sofa!" she demanded, pulling down her knickers.

I was completely her servant as I swiftly sat, my cock begging to please her as she opened her legs and straddled me, easing my bursting shaft inside her and writhing frantically, squealing, screaming as she hit the heights of her orgasm. I pumped her with every fibre of my being, in a frenzy of shuddering ecstasy.

Our desires didn't stop there. Soon we were upstairs in the bedroom, exploring and shafting in ways that I'd only ever seen in under-the-counter porno magazines. By two o'clock in the morning I was exhausted, unable to keep satisfying Barbara's insatiable sexual appetite.

I laid on the bed, flat on my back. Barbara got up and stood looking down at me.

"You'll just have to get more practise and improve your stamina," she laughed. I hardly had the energy to smile.

"I'll get dressed and go now."

She looked beautiful in her nakedness.

"But you might be seen leaving," my lust had fled. Fear now gripped me.

"It's okay. I walked to the wood. There's no car outside and it's still dark."

"But Malcolm. He'll wonder where you've been?"

"He's away. Don't worry. No-one will know."

"What does he do?" I was curious.

"Runs his own business as a management consultant. He's at a conference. I run the office at our house. General admin, keeping accounts, chasing sales leads, doing all the back-up."

Despite her reassurance he wouldn't know, I felt troubled. She left the bedroom to collect her clothes.

As well as the fear of discovery, I was also consumed with yet more guilt. The last time I'd had sex with Barbara, I believed that Alison wasn't interested in me. That there was no future in a relationship. Now we were together, and I'd betrayed her. My cheap thrill fun was over. I had a heavy heart. There was no firm commitment between Alison and me, but nevertheless I felt a heel.

After a few minutes of resting a little longer I went downstairs to say goodnight to Barbara. But she'd gone.

CHAPTER 8

I WOKE in the morning still feeling dreadful about betraying Alison by having secret sex with her sister.

As I half-heartedly ate breakfast cereal and drank a cup of tea, my thoughts turned to the other event of the previous night. The conversation between Rupert and Josh in the wood.

They were definitely searching for that cursed sword which had been used so wickedly in the past to kill innocents. I had an urge to probe further. To see if I could coax a bit more information from Rupert. Not so much in words, but perhaps through his reaction. I decided to go and see him at the bookshop on the pretext of dropping in for a chat.

He was placing some books on a stand when I entered the premises. There were no customers. There rarely seemed to be when I visited the place. No wonder he was desperate for trade.

"Just passing," I said, as he turned to see who was entering.

"I don't know how all those authors ever manage to finish their books," I joked, pointing to some of the titles on display. "Inspiration seems to flee whenever I sit down to write."

"It's ninety-nine percent perspiration and one percent inspiration," Rupert smiled.

"I think that's for being a genius," I replied. "Way out of my league." The banter helped to ease the suspicious atmosphere that had fallen between us last time we met.

"Shopping?" Rupert glanced at the bag I was holding to buy some provisions later.

"Yes, shortly. I just popped in to see if you'd had any luck locating where the sword is buried?" I was curious to see his reaction to my question.

"No, I've no idea." His reply was deadpan. "I'm not sure it's anywhere to be found now. Lost in legends and time I think."

"And you've never heard anything more about it?" he asked. Now I could tell he was studying my reaction.

"No," I lied, hoping my reply was convincing. It was difficult to tell with Rupert. How much he knew. How much he didn't. The knowledge in his eyes ran mysterious and deep.

I changed tack.

"I remember reading somewhere in the book you lent me, that someone had suggested the sword might be buried under a memorial stone at the chapel in the wood."

The reaction in Rupert's face was immediate. Puzzled, suspicious. He stared at me curiously.

"Yes, I've read that too. But it isn't suggested by the author in the book I loaned to you. I only discovered it in another book I came across a few days ago. Which book did you see it in?"

Now Rupert was analysing my reaction. Rounding on me. I couldn't say I'd been spying on him and Josh in the wood last night. That I'd overheard them talking about their search under a memorial stone. Or perhaps I should. Just to confront him.

The decision was taken from me. The phone in the back office started ringing.

"Just a moment." Rupert left to answer it. I wondered if I should leave. My fears about him were growing deeper. If he was up to something bad with Josh, they might be prepared to silence anyone interfering with their plans. Rupert didn't strike me as an aggressive man, but Josh was different. I felt certain he wouldn't hesitate in arranging my 'disappearance' and burying me in the wood if it came to it.

I prepared to leave when Rupert re-appeared from the back office.

"I've got to go out for ten minutes," he said. "Would you mind holding the fort for a while? If anyone comes in, tell them I'll be back shortly."

The decision seemed to be made for me. He swiftly left without waiting for a reply.

I waited for a few minutes and as the time passed my curiosity grew. The urge gripped me to take a sneak look in the back room of the shop. I glanced out the shop window to see no-one was approaching and quickly walked round the counter and opened the door.

On the office desk an open book rested among a scattering of documents and papers. The book looked extremely old. Leatherbound with the edges frayed by use and time.

I glanced at the two pages on view. They contained words written in a foreign text that looked like Latin, but I was no language scholar and couldn't translate it. I turned a page and saw the weird engraving of what looked like a woman in a long, black gown being burned to death at the stake. Flames leaping up to consume her. Above the image in old English script was inscribed the name BEATRICE!

The image was shocking. I knew Rupert studied the legend of Beatrice's burning, which alone didn't mean he was a bad man. But it gave me an uneasy feeling. And an air of darkness and damnation seemed to be seeping from the pages of the book into the room.

Quickly I set about opening the three drawers on each side of the desk. They were crammed with books and papers. There was no time to look through them all. Rupert could return at any moment. I glanced around the room with no idea of what I was actually looking for, just something in my mind pushing me to search. I couldn't stay much longer. How would I explain why I was in his private room if he came now?

Turning to leave, I caught sight of a shoe rack in a small alcove behind the door. There were a few pairs of shoes on the top rack and something wrapped in a white cloth on the lower one. It seemed an odd combination. I looked at my watch. Ten minutes had almost passed, but I just had to check it out.

Swiftly I unwrapped the cloth. My mouth widened in amazement. I was holding two bones. I was no expert in anatomy, but they looked remarkably like thigh bones. Small, like they were not fully grown, as in children. I almost dropped them, recoiling in horror as the thought came to me. Were these the missing thigh bones taken from the child skeletons I uncovered with Rupert in the wood? The missing bones the detective had questioned us about?

Rupert must have taken them when I wasn't looking. It wouldn't have been difficult in the darkness. Why would he want to do that?

Suddenly I had a more immediate problem. The clang of the doorbell rang out. Someone had entered the shop.

"Hello? Are you there?" It was Rupert. I was trapped. As fast as I could I wrapped the bones in the cloth and placed them back on the shoe rack. How would I explain my presence in the back office?

The door opened.

"Mark, what are you doing here?"

An excuse flashed into my head.

"Your phone rang." I glanced towards it on a shelf by the desk. "But it cut off just as I was about to answer."

He stared at me for a moment, then seemed to be happy with my explanation.

"Thanks for standing in for me. Sorry if I held you up."

I told him it was no problem. After what I'd just seen I wanted to get away from Rupert and the shop as soon as possible. The macabre discovery now troubled me. What should I do about it? I wasn't sure at that moment.

Leaving the bookshop, it was a relief to be in the fresh air again. I bought some provisions in the high street stores before starting back to the cottage.

All the while my mind was struggling to make a decision. I was convinced the two bones I'd seen in Rupert's shop belonged to the skeletons of the murdered children. It was a terrible event that occurred one hundred years previously and the bones didn't provide vital evidence to a modern day crime. But it didn't seem right. And what a strange thing to do. Take the bones and keep them in a back office.

Perhaps Rupert wanted them as some kind of tasteless memento. Or maybe he thought it might help to attract publicity in place of the sword he'd been seeking for the newspaper feature. Though a couple of thigh bones would hardly attract the world's press. Why did he want them?

I didn't like the idea of being a police informant, especially since it wasn't going to lead to the arrest of a vicious killer on the loose. The vile perpetrator of that crime had died long ago. Still, it didn't make right what Rupert had done.

The more I thought about it, the more my concern grew that something dark was being planned between him and Josh on the festival night. It was my duty to inform the authorities.

I turned and made my way back to the village police station at the other end of the high street. I'd been there before when questioned by the detective, and the building always struck me as a depressing sight. Grey, granite blocks presumably mined from the local quarry, with a black painted steel front door that could probably withhold a siege. Public rioting, however, did not look likely in this part of the world.

A young police officer stood behind the counter thumbing through a ledger. He seemed almost surprised at actually seeing a member of the public entering the station, such was the low level of crime in the area.

The officer greeted me with a smile under his cropped fair hair.

"What can I do for you sir?" he enquired. "If it's a lost cat, we've a long list of enquiries already in progress."

I wasn't sure if he was being serious or joking. I asked if Sergeant Fellows was around.

"Yes, he's just back from investigating the kidnap of an owl. If you wait a minute, I'll get him."

Now he *was* joking. Surely?

After a couple of minutes the officer returned with Sergeant Fellows, who gave me a puzzled look. I told him I had some information. He led me to an interview room.

"Have you really just got back from investigating the kidnap of an owl?" I was truly curious. The village was filled with strange ways and I could almost believe anything.

Fellows laughed.

"Was that him at the counter?"

I nodded.

"When he joined up six months ago he had visions of being rapidly selected for a top ranking job with the serious crime squad in London. Your neck of the woods." The sergeant laughed again.

"Now he realises that he's likely to get nothing more exciting round here than people reporting lost pets. I think he's going a bit loopy." Fellows was obviously amused by the thought.

"Well I don't think this ranks as serious crime," I began, "but I think I know where the missing thigh bones are being kept. The ones belonging to the child skeletons Rupert and I discovered in the wood."

My words stripped all the amusement from the sergeant's face in an instant.

Where?"

I had his complete attention. When I finished telling him where I'd seen the bones he shook his head as if something in his mind was falling into place.

He said Barbara had been to his house that morning to tell him of the conversation we'd heard between Rupert and Josh in the wood. Their search for the missing sword.

It put me on the spot for a moment, because I'd told him when he'd questioned me a day or two ago that I knew nothing about a missing sword. Would he question me further about it now?

Fortunately that didn't seem to be his concern. He was more interested in the discovery of the thigh bones.

"I would suggest from now on you stay out of this local business. I don't want you putting yourself at risk," Fellows told me in a tone that sounded ominous.

I agreed, though not entirely sure how I could entirely keep out of it without cutting my links to Alison. And I didn't want to do that. As for Barbara, she was attractive and sexy, but I could live without seeing her again. Although that could be difficult if I continued a relationship with her sister. Why was life so bloody difficult?

"Is this a confidential conversation?" I asked the sergeant.

While I felt it my duty to report what I'd seen, I was troubled about Rupert discovering I was an informant on him. Partly because it made me feel a bit of a low sneak, but more so because he was a friend of Josh's, and I could seriously end up the next person to be buried in the wood.

"Don't worry. This conversation is entirely between us," Fellows assured me. Taking some comfort from his promise, I left and returned to the cottage.

The events of the day had drained me more than I'd realised. The plan was to have a short rest on the sofa, then try to get on with my writing. It came as a total surprise when I awoke to loud knocking on the front door. I looked at my watch. It was seven in the evening. I'd slept far longer than intended. I got up quickly and opened the door.

Rupert confronted me.

"You piece of shit!" he yelled angrily.

The fury and disgust in his face scared me. This was a slice of temper short of attacking me. Sixth sense told me why he was here and I felt Sergeant Fellows had betrayed me. But I feigned innocence.

"What have I done?" I protested.

"You know what you've done," Rupert snarled. "It was you, wasn't it? You told Sergeant Fellows I had the thigh bones in my office."

"Did I? Did he tell you that?" I stuttered

"Of course he bloody didn't tell me," Rupert raged. "Come on. You know it was you who told Fellows. At least have the guts to confess."

His last words riled me.

"The guts to confess! You stole the bones of the murdered children and hid them away like a dirty little thief. And you've got the bloody cheek to tell me to have some guts!" Now I was raging. "Then you come pointing the finger at me. What do you want with their bones anyway? You're bloody perverted!"

Rupert stepped back. His face changed from anger to a cold, hard stare.

"If you hadn't left the book on my desk open at a different page and made such a hash of re-wrapping the bones in the cloth, I wouldn't have suspected you," he told me calmly. "And there are two phones in my office. The one you said had been ringing is disconnected. That was just a lie."

Now I was on the back foot again.

"The sergeant has charged me with stealing dead body parts and the bones have been confiscated for return to the coroner's office," Rupert explained.

That seemed fair enough to me.

"Did you tell Sergeant Fellows I was in the wood by the chapel looking for a sword last night?" he asked accusingly.

I could honestly deny that, remembering Barbara had told the officer about the event.

"No," I replied. Rupert seemed to believe me.

"I'm warning you," he pointed his finger aggressively at me like a weapon poised to attack. "Keep out of this. You are treading in dangerous territory. Things you don't understand. Stick to your fiction – or you may become the main character in a real story that ends in your death!"

His warning chilled me. The once mild-mannered man, who I thought wouldn't hurt a fly, had put the fear of God in me. In a strange way, it was more frightening than a threat from a man who was naturally violent like Josh. I closed the door as he walked away.

Now I was racked with yet more doubts and confusion. The prospect of catching the first train home tomorrow morning was tempting. But I wasn't going to be forced to run away. And there was Alison. I wanted her to be an important part of my life.

I went into the kitchen and poured myself a glass of wine, sorely in need of a drink. The disconnected phone in the living room started ringing. The sound filled me with dread. Those long dead children were trying to reach me again. I looked around the kitchen sensing unseen spirits looking at me, knowing my every movement, my conversations, all the intimate details of my life. It was driving me insane. I'd had enough.

"That fucking phone," I shouted, rushing into the living room, picking it up and smashing it into the wall, watching the handset and holder separate and scatter across the floor. That was the end of hearing from those undead spirits again.

Then I heard a faint voice. It came from the handset, which was cracked but still attached by its cord to the holder. Reluctantly I lifted it from the floor.

"Go away! Just go away!" I shouted into the mouthpiece. The voice persisted. It was the girl.

"Don't be fooled," she said, repeating the words, "don't be fooled." The line went dead.

"Don't be fooled?" I repeated to myself. Fooled about what? I'd been fooled by just about everything in this accursed place. I'd fooled myself about coming here for peace and quiet.

I picked up the phone and replaced it on the side table. It was a solid piece of black plastic and apart from the handset crack had suffered no other damage. If it rang again, I'd find a hammer and smash it to pieces.

Perhaps for now though, I'd be left undisturbed. My hope was short lived.

No sooner had I returned to the kitchen to drink my glass of wine when there was a knock at the front door. I decided to ignore the call, and sat down to finish the drink.

After a few more knocks I heard the letterbox flap squeak open.

"Are you in?" a woman's voice echoed down the hall. It was Barbara.

Desirable as she was, another night of secret sex was not what I wanted right now. The woman was all consuming and any further involvement with her was likely to land me in yet more local complications.

"I know you're in, I can see the light," her voice echoed through the letterbox opening again. I'd have to answer and just send her away as quickly as possible. Yet even at that moment my resolve was rapidly starting to dissolve at the memory of her beautiful body and desires.

My growing urge was immediately flattened as I opened the door. Barbara stood there with fiancée Malcolm by her side.

"We were just passing and thought we'd drop in to invite you to a party we're holding after the Beatrice bonfire on Saturday night." Barbara smiled encouragingly.

Malcolm's face was deadpan. No welcome. Devoid of emotion. I sensed he was sizing me up as his rival in love.

I wasn't sure if I wanted to join the revelry. Barbara detected my reluctance.

"You've got to come," she insisted. "It'll be great fun. Music and dancing. Alison's coming." Barbara knew that would be the hook to entice me.

"Can we come in?" she asked, hardly waiting to be invited inside as she began entering. I stood aside. Malcolm's straight face told me he wasn't keen to make any greater acquaintance with me. The feeling was entirely mutual.

"You must get ever so lonely at night," Barbara continued, completely ignoring the cold front between me and Malcolm. She was a shrew. She knew perfectly well I hadn't been lonely on the nights we'd spent shagging each other. But I played along.

"I'm okay. It gives me plenty of time to write."

"We're going to a nightclub," Barbara announced as we entered the living room. "But I wouldn't mind a glass of wine if you have any."

She stood there, her shining fair hair folding into that proud, statuesque neck. Her innocent face only undone by the mischievous eyes that briefly caught mine. She wore a low-cut cream top and crimson mini-skirt, the shortest I'd yet seen, revealing those wonderfully shapely thighs and legs in dark tights.

I could swear she was teasing me in front of Malcolm when she turned and bent over to straighten a cushion on the sofa, giving me a quick glimpse of her matching crimson panties.

Even with Malcolm present, I could feel my growing erection. But for now it was necessarily suppressed with frustration. God, I wanted to take her there and then.

"I've got a bottle of red wine in the kitchen," I said, as much a distraction from my own lustful thoughts as a drink offer.

"Perfect," Barbara replied.

"We can't stay long." Malcolm interrupted.

"Just a quickie," said Barbara, giving me a sly wink.

I went to the kitchen and brought back two glasses of wine on a tray.

"Cheers," said Barbara, lifting the glass to her lips. "Here's to you becoming a famous author."

Fame at my present rate of writing seemed a universe away.

"You're looking unhappy," Barbara frowned. She could see I wanted to unload my mental burden, but I felt reluctant with her fiancée standing beside her in his smart, dark suit looking every bit as if he would rather be somewhere else.

"It's okay. Malcolm and me have no secrets between us. Come on, tell me what's the matter?"

It was amazing that Barbara could stand there and say there were no secrets between Malcolm and herself, without the slightest sign of guilt about us having sex together. But on this occasion there was no reason why Malcolm shouldn't know what was troubling me.

"I had a threatening visit from Rupert this evening." I explained what had happened.

Barbara appeared shocked.

"I didn't know he'd stolen the children's thigh bones! What on earth could he want them for?"

I confessed I had no idea. But told her I felt something strange was being hatched between Rupert and Josh.

"Well, Sergeant Bob Fellows has plenty of information to keep an eye on that pair," she replied.

"Josh is a nasty piece of work. It wouldn't surprise me one bit if he was planning something bad for the Burning Beatrice festival night." Malcolm spoke for the first time since he'd arrived.

"And Rupert has an unhealthy interest in the occult," he continued. "Barbara told me she'd overheard a conversation between him and Josh in the woods the other night. Looking for the sword used to slay those poor children all those years ago."

Obviously Barbara had shared that piece of information with Malcolm, though hopefully without letting him know I'd been with her and we'd returned to my cottage for the night. On balance, I think he would have had more to say if he knew. Two-timing was yet another complication in my life, and every moment I was beginning to regret it.

"Anyway. You must come to our party on Saturday night. In fancy dress." Barbara finished her drink. "Alison tells me you've tried on the wizard's costume and you look magical in it."

I smiled and thought of the hot fitting session I'd enjoyed with her.

"Watch out! She's got her eye on you," Barbara laughed, bending forward to kiss me on the cheek.

I caught Malcolm's gaze. He did not look happy with her lips contacting me.

"Must be going," she said.

Malcolm put down his glass of wine. He hadn't touched a drop. And he didn't say goodbye as they left.

I closed the door. The yearning for peace grew stronger. It seemed my life was becoming yet more and more webbed in the undercurrent of emotions and fears throbbing in this village. It would hardly be great going to a party where the host's fiancée hated you.

I sat on the sofa to rest for a moment. Not a few minutes had passed when I heard the squeak of the letterbox opening and the sound of something dropping to the hall floor.

"What now?" I thought. The postman doesn't come at this hour. My tiredness told me to leave it. My curiosity won.

It was a hastily scribbled note on a scrap of paper that took me a moment or so to read.

"Come to the old chapel now. The future waits," it said.

What the hell did that mean? Who wrote it?

I took the note into the living and dropped it on the sofa. I poured myself another glass of wine. The prospect of going into the wood in darkness filled me with dread after the last close encounter with Rupert and Josh. And the old chapel had an aura of creepiness, sadness about it. Of lost spirits wandering endlessly in the vain hope of finding rest.

But if I could really learn of the future as the note said, perhaps it would lead me to discovering the plot being hatched for some evil event at the Beatrice festival. On the other hand it could be a way of Rupert and Josh luring me into a trap.

Once again curiosity took the reins. I had to go. But prepared.

I slipped a paring knife from the kitchen into my denim jacket pocket just in case of attack. Grabbing a torch from the counter, I opened the door and stepped outside.

Moonlight glowed through a gauze layer of cloud spread across the sky, casting a blurred outline of my shadow as I walked along the gravel drive towards the lane. The tops of the trees in the wood opposite hovered in silvery silhouettes. All was still. Not a breath of breeze. My footsteps made the only sound.

A short distance down the lane I reached the footpath into the woodland and with the torchlight picked my way through the surrounding darkness. I knew the way from here.

Occasionally the hazy moonlight broke through the canopy of trees, soon lighting the derelict outline of the old chapel as I approached the clearing in the wood.

Instinct urged me to return as quickly as possible to the cottage. Any vestige of courage I'd fooled myself into possessing now fled with every passing second. A dangerous, eerie atmosphere drifted all around. But curiosity drove me on. I saw a breach in the wire fence surrounding the building.

I called out.

"Anyone here?"

The sound echoed and faded. No reply. I stooped down and made my way through the fence gap. Stepping over the rubble and weeds, I entered the collapsed opening into the chapel.

"Anyone here?" I repeated, shining the torch across the ruins of the floor. Still no reply. Either I was on a fool's errand or this really was a trap. I guided the torch beam across the crumbling walls. Nothing but disintegration caught the light.

Then two figures glowing in the darkness caught my eye. They sat against the wall at the far end of the chapel on the raised floor where the altar once stood.

My God! It was the children!

A silver sword rested on the wall between them, the tip touching the ground.

"We cannot walk. Bones have been stolen from us!" the children cried out.

The chill of death ran through my body.

"Don't be fooled!" the children screamed at me.

"What are you doing here?" a voice boomed from behind. I swung round. My torch lit the furious face of Josh. He advanced shining a flashlight at me.

"I warned you to stay out of this. You're asking to die!"

A horrifying screech of laughter broke out. I swung round again, dropping the torch in panic.

The children were gone. A figure in a long, black gown stood beside the sword. It lifted the weapon and seemed to glide across the floor, advancing and raising the blade to strike. I wanted to run. Take out my knife in defence. I couldn't move. Petrified. The figure was almost on me. It stopped.

"Ah! Let me see your lovely neck," a woman's shrill voice commanded. I couldn't resist. I held my head back.

Now I saw the face. Withered, scorched and blackened as if by fire, sunken eyes rolling with a smile of deathly evil. But as I stood transfixed, I could see further into those eyes. The indistinct image of a beautiful young woman somehow trapped in the vicious depths.

The hag before me held the blade steady, ready to slice my throat with a strike.

Suddenly the children's voices broke the air.

"Your end approaches!" they cried.

The hag turned round. The spell broke. I could move. Stumbling across the rubble, floundering in darkness I ran as fast as I could from the hellish place, guided only by the shafts of moonlight spreading through the trees.

I was nearly out of the wood when the hag appeared in front of me, raising the sword again.

"No! Don't kill me!" I yelled, and woke on the sofa, sweating, shaking, trembling in terror.

The only relief lay in realising I'd fallen asleep and had a terrible nightmare. The sense of foreboding and dread that something evil was yet come lived on.

I stood up feeling exhausted, in need of proper rest. Though God knows, I feared going to sleep again in case another terrifying dream came to haunt me.

Stepping into the hall to climb the stairs to bed, I noticed a scrap of paper on the floor beneath the letterbox. I picked it up. It was blank. I was right about something dropping through the letterbox, but there was no message written on it about going to the wood. I needed rest, I couldn't cope with any more puzzles right now. Placing the scrap of paper on the kitchen table I went upstairs.

CHAPTER 9

SUNLIGHT flooded the bedroom as I opened the curtains to a new morning. The treetops bordering the wood across the lane were no longer coated in mysterious, silver moonlight. Now they basked radiantly, leaves swaying in a gentle breeze, the spirits of the night chased away.

Last night's awful dream remained a vivid memory. My subconscious was desperately trying to tell me something, of that I was certain. But the answer remained locked away.

In the kitchen, I picked up the scrap of paper that I'd put on the table before going to bed and checked to make sure it really was blank. That remained the case. The scribbled words about the wood rendezvous were just a figment of my dream.

What now puzzled me was the texture of the paper. It seemed very thick and slightly browned with age. The jagged tear along one edge indicated it had been hurriedly ripped from a larger piece of – then it struck me – parchment. This paper came from long ago. Possibly a century or two earlier.

I looked closer, holding it up to the light streaming through the kitchen window. There appeared to be a very slight indentation on the surface, as if someone had written something on another piece of parchment resting on it. I couldn't work out what it might read.

Then a thought came to me. A game I'd played as a boy 'detecting' secret writing. A way to reveal the impression left below on a written notepad.

I found a pencil in the sitting room chest of drawers and ever so carefully began to rub the lead lightly across the indents on the parchment. They began to be revealed as the surrounding surface drew them out in contrasting highlight. I struggled to read the text. It seemed to be written in italics. An old style of handwriting.

Holding the parchment up to the light again gave it greater contrast. I couldn't swear to it, but after a minute or two of eye strain I'm sure I made out the words 'condemned to burning at the stake for witchcraft'. The impression was too faint to complete the line, though below it there appeared to be something resembling an indistinct signature.

The triumph of my detection was of little comfort. Who had posted the scrap of parchment through my door? Did it cause me to have that terrible dream through some strange supernatural link? Was it from a pile of parchments associated with Beatrice being condemned to death two hundred years ago?

The only person I knew who had studied the event in detail, and had access to books and possibly documents from the time was Rupert. What was his motive? He'd stolen the murdered children's thigh bones. Was he persecuting me through black magic? Revenge for me telling Sergeant Fellows of his macabre stash of the bones?

But surely Rupert didn't have supernatural powers? Once again my mind was in turmoil.

Placing the scrap of parchment back on the kitchen table, I walked across to the counter to make a cup of tea and pour milk on my cereal. After a few moments I could smell burning. Turning swiftly round, I was shocked to see the parchment had burst into flames and was fast flaking into ash.

I grabbed a damp cloth to smother the flames, but by then there was practically nothing left bar a tiny piece with a blackened edge.

The parchment must have self-combusted. The legend that the child murderer Samuel Holroyd had died through spontaneous combustion flashed into my mind. Now I was gripped with fear again. Something paranormal was taking over my life and it felt like a hovering shroud of doom descending on me.

A voice in my head was shouting 'get away before it's too late!' But I couldn't run and be a coward. My heart told me to stay and fight. Defeat this enemy at any price. 'You're a bloody fool' another voice in my mind echoed.

****

FOR now my writing definitely took a back seat. The frightening position I found myself in became the priority. The answer lived somewhere in my brain, of that I felt certain. But the more I strained to grasp at the clues, the more the solution drifted away.

I'd just finished washing up a stack of dirty crockery when there was a knock at the front door. The kitchen clock pointed to just after seven. It seemed a bit early for callers. Perhaps the postman was delivering a package. I tossed the tea-towel onto the table and went to answer the call.

Alison stood there wearing a smart, navy-blue jacket and skirt. She looked radiant. Her welcoming, friendly smile driving away my dark mood.

"Just thought I'd pop round on my way to work," she said.

I invited her in.

"Can't stop long. Just wanted to see how you are and remind you to come to the shop after five tomorrow for your wizard outfit."

During my stay in the village, I'd seen piles of wood for the Beatrice bonfire gradually building into a stack in a local field ready for the big night.

I made Alison a cup of tea in the kitchen.

"You look a bit pale? Is everything okay?" she asked.

I told her about my discovery of the children's thigh bones at Rupert's bookshop. The nasty visit from him and the strange dream I'd had.

"And this," I pointed to a small piece of ash still on the kitchen table which I'd missed while clearing away the burnt parchment remains.

Alison was readily sympathetic to me about Rupert's aggressiveness and strange behaviour, but when I told her the scrap of parchment had burst into flames, she looked at me doubtfully. A piece of ash was no proof of the event.

"Are you sure you're not reading too much into it all?" She sounded concerned for my mental health.

"I've been threatened by Josh and now Rupert!" anger rose in me. "That's not reading too much into it."

"I know. That is bad. But they're only threats. Just distance yourself from it," Alison was trying to keep the mood calm.

"You're right," I agreed, after thinking about it for a moment or two.

"Barbara came round with Malcolm and invited me to a party after the bonfire," I changed the subject. "She said you were coming."

"Yes. We'll all be dressed in our wizard and witch costumes. Should be good fun."

A thought occurred to me.

"Did Barbara tell you we saw Rupert and Josh searching for the missing sword in the wood the other night? The one that disappeared from the attic in your house?"

"No. But then I haven't seen Barbara for a while."

I told her how we'd literally bumped into each other in the darkness and overheard the two men talking. Alison was surprised.

"And what have you done about it?"

"Barbara reported it to Sergeant Fellows the next day."

"Can't imagine he'll be able to do much," Alison replied with a cynical smile.

"Anyway, I better get on to work. Can I use your bathroom before I go?"

I nodded and cleared away the teacups as Alison headed upstairs.

When she returned she approached me with a strange, quizzical look.

"Do you wear bracelets?" she asked.

I returned her quizzical gaze.

"Of course not."

"While I was in the bathroom, there was a towel on the floor in the corner. I picked it up to put it in the linen bin. Underneath I saw this."

Alison brought her right hand from behind her back, holding a silver bracelet.

"This looks exactly like one that Barbara wears. I know because I was with her on a shopping trip when she bought it."

I could feel my cheeks redden and grow hot.

"Did she stay the night after you 'bumped' into her in the wood?" Alison demanded.

"Well..." I faltered. "Yes. She was tired," I heard the unconvincing explanation pouring out of my mouth. I just knew Alison could see guilt all over my face.

"Then shall I return the bracelet to her, or will you?" she asked.

I was speechless.

"I'll leave it here," Alison placed it on the kitchen table, "so you can make up your mind."

Her last words struck. A warning shot. I must decide between Alison or her sister where my affections truly lay.

I reached out to assure Alison that she was the woman I wanted to be with, but she backed away and walked out of the kitchen into the hallway.

"I'll see you tomorrow, just after five." She opened the front door and left.

Now I felt absolutely terrible. My relationship with her was in a fragile balance. Strangely I was glad I hadn't been able to fool Alison with a lie, pathetic though my cover-up must have looked. I didn't want any more secrets to come between us. There were too many secrets in this place and I began to realise how damaging deception could become. My dread now was a big falling out between the sisters, with me as the main target.

Alison had left the front door open. I closed it and turned to go back to the kitchen.

I nearly had a heart attack!

The hag I'd seen in my nightmare dream stood in the hallway. Only feet away. She grimaced through that withered, fire-blackened face, her long dark gown draped on the floor.

I stood transfixed in terror. The hag raised her arm and pointed a long, skeletal finger at me.

"Soon you will be mine," she said, tossing her head back and breaking into hellish laughter, relishing some diabolical fate that awaited me. Then she was gone.

My first instinct was to flee from the cottage. I staggered into the kitchen and slumped on a chair, hoping it was yet another bad dream. But this time I was already awake.

Now I'd really seen the hag, and I had no doubt the apparition was Beatrice!

As I sat resting, trying to recover my wits and get my base instincts of panic under control, I caught sight of Barbara's silver bracelet, which Alison had left on the kitchen table.

I picked up the trinket and noticed there was a small name plate in the links. But instead of a name or initials, I could see engraved on the surface a small circle with a triangle inside. The symbol stirred something in my memory, but I couldn't place where I'd seen it before.

The image of the witch in the hallway had left me badly shaken. Entering the hallway to reach the front door, I dared hardly look back to the spot where the hag had stood, but curiosity forced me to turn.

Down the hallway the door into the living room was open. I could see the furniture inside and the back garden patio door behind. All appeared normal, but uncannily still. Stepping into the front garden, the breeze felt refreshing. I tried to concentrate on other matters.

A letter had arrived from my mother yesterday saying my father was making good progress after his minor heart attack, and he'd soon be returning to work. That news was heart warming. Thank God he was recovering.

I'd never told my mother about the difficulties and odd events I'd been experiencing in the village. As far as she and my father were concerned, I too was making good progress. She also told me my sister, Helen, who'd emigrated to Australia three years ago, was planning to come over for a family visit in the New Year.

My happier thoughts were suddenly blown to pieces. Barbara's bracelet on the kitchen table. The circle and triangle engraved on it. I remembered where I'd seen the symbol before.

****

ALISON finished her packed lunch in the rest room at the clothes shop then returned to the sales counter.

Mrs Collins, the owner, asked her to re-arrange a dress display in the shop window and disappeared out back to eat her lunch.

A few minutes later the doorbell clanged loudly as Malcolm came speeding into the premises.

"Alison," he called out urgently.

She was stooping, arranging a dress on a mannequin. His cry made her spring up swiftly, knocking over an arrangement of necklaces on a stand beside her. She was surprised to see him.

"Quick!" Malcolm beckoned. "Your mother's been taken ill. She's in the local hospital. I'll drive you there."

Alison went numb with shock. Panic shot through her.

"God!" she cried, stepping back into the shop. "What's wrong?"

"Not sure. She just collapsed. They're running tests. Quick."

The noise brought Mrs Collins from the back room.

"My mother's been taken to hospital. I've got to go," Alison told her. She followed Malcolm to his red Cortina car parked out side. They climbed in and he drove off at speed.

"Is she conscious? What happened?" Alison was close to tears with worry.

"I just know she was taken to hospital. I'd called round to pick up some letters Barbara had left there and a neighbour said your mum had collapsed and was in the local hospital."

"Does Barbara know?" Alison was frantic.

"Yes. She's driving there now."

Alison was a bundle of nerves. The fear that her mother might die. Might already be dead! If the worst had happened, she didn't know how she'd cope. Not knowing what was wrong. That was awful.

Her mind was totally absorbed with dread and it was only after a few minutes that she became aware of the passing surroundings.

"This isn't the way to the hospital." She looked around, puzzled.

"It's a short cut," Malcolm replied.

For a moment she believed him. But Alison knew the area like the back of her hand. It wasn't a short cut. This road went nowhere near the hospital. She recognised exactly where led.

****

I WENT back to the kitchen. The memory of where I'd seen that circle and triangle symbol on Barbara's bracelet had become crystal clear.

It was one of the symbols shown in the book Rupert had loaned me about the area's myths and legends.

I picked up the bracelet from the kitchen table and studied the symbol again. In the book it was associated with the ring that Beatrice had worn. Some of the villagers, who Beatrice had helped cure of illnesses in those times, knew she had worn the ring as a symbol of healing. They also believed she had been wrongly accused of witchcraft. But they dared not speak up for fear of being accused of witchcraft themselves.

As she burned at the stake and cried out her curse, they were convinced the symbol had turned to represent evil.

I thought it highly unlikely the original ring could be around now. Barbara must have had a copy of the symbol made for the bracelet. But why would she want a bracelet with that symbol on it? Did she know what it represented?

The centenary of Beatrice's death was being celebrated tomorrow. I felt compelled to walk to Barbara's cottage right now and ask her. But if her fiancée, Malcolm, was there it would be difficult explaining how Barbara had left her bracelet at my place without raising his suspicions of our intimacy.

I'd have to ask Barbara when we were alone, though at that moment I couldn't think where and when. And I couldn't ask Alison to question her sister about it. That would probably set off more fireworks than the ones at the festival. Best thing would be to try and draw Barbara aside and ask her at the bonfire celebration tomorrow.

Not a great strategy. But all I could do for now.

Settled with a makeshift plan, I decided to concentrate on my novel writing again. For several hours I tried, but ended up discarding sheet after sheet from the typewriter until a heap of paper covered the floor beside me.

Too many distracting thoughts. Frequently I glanced nervously towards the open doorway of the living room, fearing the witch Beatrice might make another unwelcome appearance. The cottage was seriously giving me the creeps.

By six o'clock in the evening I'd had enough, and the upset Alison had suffered finding her sister's bracelet in the bathroom weighed on my mind. I was frightened of losing her. She needed my reassurance that I loved her and no-one else. That was it. I'd go and see her now to pledge my loyalty to her. She'd have finished work and was probably back home.

The thought of encountering her mother, Emma, who'd taken against me, was daunting. But hell. I wanted Alison, not her mother.

I set off for Alison's house. A gift of flowers for her would be a good start, but the local florist in the high street was closed. Approaching the house, I prayed Alison would answer the door and not her mother. She was likely to slam it in my face.

I knocked and waited. No answer. I knocked again louder, thinking no-one had heard. Still no answer. As I stood waiting a door across the road opened. An elderly woman wearing a brown pinafore appeared.

"Mrs Carpenter's staying with friends tonight," she called.

"Do you mean Emma?" I asked.

"Yes. She'll be back tomorrow."

"It's her daughter, Alison, I'm looking for," I explained.

"Don't know where she is. Who are you?"

"A friend."

The woman looked at me suspiciously. She obviously monitored the street through the lace curtain at her front window. She turned and went back into the house.

I felt empty. I'd so wanted to re-kindle the bond between Alison and me that I'd so carelessly thrown away to temptation.

Alison was probably out with friends for the evening. Now I worried she was giving up on me. Even now a good looking bloke could be making her laugh. Dancing with her at a club in the nearby town. Now I'd blown it all. No novel. Lost love and a heap of village troubles dumped on me. Why did I ever come to this place?

With a heavy heart I began my walk back to the cottage. The high street was quiet. Shops closed. Everyone at home enjoying their evening meals, watching TV, living a normal life.

As I neared Rupert's bookshop the clang of the doorbell rang out. Rupert and Josh were leaving the premises. I was only several feet away and instinctively ducked inside the porch of the shop next door, hardly daring to breathe less they heard me.

Josh appeared hunched as if shielding something. He approached the black Austin van parked outside while Rupert opened the back doors. Josh place the object he was furtively holding inside the van. I caught a quick glimpse. It was a shotgun!

Rupert went back inside the shop and returned hunched, secretively trying to shield whatever he was carrying in his arms. He handed it to Josh who swiftly placed it in the van. I couldn't be sure, but I swear it looked like a silver cylinder with a small hose attached.

"Go carefully with that," Rupert spoke in a hushed voice to his companion. "It's taken me years to perfect the potion and it's deadly dangerous."

Josh closed the back doors of the van then drove it away. Rupert returned to his shop.

I didn't want to risk walking past. Rupert might see me and become suspicious. There was an alleyway nearby. It led to a path behind the high street where I could get back to the cottage. I went that way.

The two men were obviously conspiring to do something terrible. But who could I tell? Perhaps I should contact Sergeant Fellows? But I hadn't any faith he would do much.

Maybe confronting Rupert right now might prevent them from carrying out whatever evil plan they had in mind. Josh was a dangerous man though, and it seemed Rupert was more fiery inside than his calm exterior revealed.

A short time later I was back at the cottage and felt a great sense of relief closing the front door to the outside world. It was brief relief, as the thought of Beatrice's unwelcome appearance came back to me, and I frequently looked over my shoulder fearing she was standing behind.

I heated some tomato soup and dipped pieces of dry bread into the creamy liquid, softening it enough to eat. If I wasn't a famous author yet, I was beginning to sample the meagre diet of early struggle. Money was running low.

Attempting to write more of my book, the words just wouldn't come. After a couple of hours I decided to get some rest and went upstairs to bed.

The wind outside had begun to strengthen with howling gusts rattling the cottage's old sash windows. The single light bulb hanging from a cord in the bedroom shone dimly. The bed and nearby dark brown wardrobe seemed steeped in a shadowy gloom. The hands of the clock on the bedside table pointed to just after ten-thirty.

I took off my shoes and crossed to the window to close the curtains against the wind and darkness beyond.

Then I caught sight of them. The children standing together in the front garden below. They stared up at me, melancholy in their gaze, softly glowing in the night.

I jumped back. Shocked. I was being haunted. I couldn't live with the fear of apparitions suddenly appearing for much longer. I looked out the window again hoping the vision was just my overwrought imagination.

But no! The children were still there. Staring. Then the disconnected phone in the living room began to ring, echoing up the stairs. No. I wouldn't answer it. Why won't they all go away? Leave me in peace!

Suddenly the children turned as if in fear. The phone stopped ringing. A figure was approaching them in the darkness. The boy and girl disappeared and standing where they had stood was Beatrice the witch. She looked up at me and I could see a grin appearing on her distorted, fire-blackened face. Then she began to approach the cottage door.

The witch was coming for me.

A blast of wind struck the window which rattled with such force I thought it would cave-in. I leapt across to the bedroom door to slam it shut against the approaching evil. I heard the front door below swing open with an echoing creak. My heart was pounding, almost bursting through my chest.

"Hello," a woman's voice travelled upwards. "Is there anyone in?"

Was Beatrice trying to fool me, lure me? The voice sounded friendly. Not threatening. I felt cold sweat on my brow.

"Hello. Is anyone in?" the woman's voice repeated.

I could hear footsteps moving along the hallway. This couldn't be Beatrice. It sounded like a normal human voice. Normal steps. I opened the bedroom door and glanced down the stairs. A woman glanced up.

"Hello. I'm Mrs Clark. I live in the cottage next door."

In the time I'd been at Deersmoor, I'd never met my nearest neighbour. Occasionally I'd nodded greeting to a man who lived in the next cottage when he'd been working in the front garden. Now I presumed this must be his wife. I came down the stairs to see a middle-aged woman with a kindly smile standing in the hallway.

"Sorry to disturb you. The door was ajar so I came in to tell you..." she paused. "Are you alright?" She looked concerned.

"No. I'm okay," I replied, so grateful to see her and not an evil spirit with intent to harm me.

"Just a bit of a headache," I said. She seemed reassured.

"I came round to tell you a large branch on a tree in your garden has split away in the wind and is resting on the wooden fence between us. If it's left it will break the fence."

"I'll see to it," I replied.

"Oh no, it's too heavy for one person to deal with. My husband will come round. He's got a saw and equipment to deal with it," Mrs Clark insisted.

I was glad of the generous offer since I was wondering how I'd remove a large tree branch from a fence right now.

Her husband, Bill, was a stocky, muscular man who in truth did most of the heavy duty work. Perched on a ladder secured by rope round the tree trunk, he sawed through the branch and manoeuvred it off the fence in the beam of a searchlight. The strong wind by now had dropped to a breeze.

"I do this sort of work all the time," Bill told me amid grunts of his labouring. "Building jobs, house and shop refits round the village. Tidying up fallen and broken trees in the local wood."

I said I'd met the village woodkeeper, Josh. That he didn't seem to like me much.

"I don't think he likes anyone," Bill replied. "He's a miserable sod."

I wondered if I should mention my suspicions about him, but it didn't feel the right moment. Bill was breathing heavily as he hoisted the weighty branch off the fence with my token contribution to the lifting. The man had the strength of an ox.

He laid the broken branch in the garden.

"I'll come round tomorrow and cut it up with the chainsaw. Make some good logs for your fire come winter," said Bill.

"No. You have them," I replied. "I'll probably be back in London by then."

He thanked me for the fuel payment in trade for his labours. I helped him carry back the equipment to his house and we said goodnight.

The brief company of Bill and his wife had lifted my spirits and the terror of the spectres I'd seen earlier receded. Now I wanted more than ever to return home to the bustle and familiar surroundings I'd left behind for this village.

****

NEXT morning Bill came round to slice the broken tree branch. Soon the roaring motor of the chainsaw had reduced it to logs ready for a cosy fire.

As I helped him lift the wood into a wheelbarrow to cart to his house, we were able to hear ourselves speak again.

"My wife thinks something's troubling you," Bill came out with it plainly.

"Does she?" I asked defensively.

"Yes. She said you looked like you'd seen a ghost when she came round last night." He lifted the handles of the loaded wheelbarrow and started to push it towards the back garden side path leading to the drive.

I didn't know how to reply. I had seen a ghost. Ghosts. But I couldn't confess it. He'd think me mad. I followed him out to the drive and along a path leading to his own garden. As we approached the gate his wife came out to greet me. She wore a floral dress, complementing her bright, sunny smile.

"Are you feeling better today?" she asked.

"Fine," I said, stopping for a moment as Bill continued to push the wheelbarrow through the open gate into their garden.

"I saw her too," Mrs Clark announced.

I wasn't sure what she meant. She read the confusion in my face.

"Beatrice the witch," she told me in a matter of fact voice, as if there was nothing unusual about it.

I was stunned. The chilling memory flooded back of that vile spectre approaching my front door in the night.

"Beatrice saw me approaching your cottage and fled back to the hell where she lives," Mrs Clark continued in a tone that held no fear at all. The woman was entirely unphased by the spectre.

"Come into the house," she invited. "You're very troubled. I can tell."

At that moment the prospect of a friend, who apparently seemed totally unmoved by the powers of the supernatural, stood as a mountain of strength to me.

I followed her into the cottage. She led me to the living room where framed family photos rested on a cabinet, chintz curtains bordered a French window overlooking the lawn and a large print of a woodland scene hung above the mantelpiece.

She invited me to sit on the brown leather armchair and after leaving for a moment came back with a pot of tea and cups on a tray, setting them on a small table.

"Tell me your troubles," she said, sitting on the leather sofa nearby and pouring the tea.

I didn't know where to start and wasn't sure if it would make any sense.

"You've seen the spirits of the children in the wood," she continued, encouraging me to open up. "I imagine it's something to do with that."

I agreed she was on the right track.

"I'm a white witch," Mrs Clark announced. "I know about these things."

A white witch! My knowledge of the paranormal was limited, but I did know a white witch was reputed to be someone with supernatural powers of good intent. I would have dismissed it all as a load of nonsense had it not been for the fact she'd seen the unearthly Beatrice without me ever saying a word to her.

"Just tell me. I will believe what others would dismiss as rubbish."

Her kindness and relaxed manner made me feel at ease. She took a sip of tea as I considered whether to tell all, and unburden myself to a stranger who had no emotional ties with me.

I described what had happened since I came to Deersmoor. Not the intimate bits, but everything else. The ghosts, the missing sword, my suspicions about Rupert and Josh and my fear something terrible was going to happen at the Burning Beatrice festival.

Mrs Clark looked thoughtful.

"Yes, the powers are gathering, I feel it," she replied, lowering her head as if considering something.

With all the distractions it had slipped my mind that the festival was tonight. If anything was going to happen it was only hours away.

"Soon you will be mine," the voice and vision of Beatrice in the hallway set my heart racing again.

"Calm down," Mrs Clark could sense my fear. "I will help you."

I wondered precisely how she could, but her confidence was infectious.

She stood up and went across to a bookshelf in the corner of the room looking for a title. Reaching out she selected a book and thumbed through the pages.

"Ah, here it is," she brought the book over to me.

"Of course, I should have realised," she said, lowering the open page for me to see and pointing to a section.

"The text is in very old English, but translated into plain words it says, '...every 100th anniversary from the burning, the witch shall rise to do evil and give those with ill intent ungodly power. A stranger will come to undo the curse of hell, but at the risk of death and eternal damnation.'"

Mrs Clark closed the book.

"This is the reprint of a text written by a spiritual guide not long after Beatrice was burned," she explained.

I was beginning to dread the thought rapidly surfacing in my brain.

"You are the stranger," she confirmed my fear.

I stood up.

"That's it. I'm catching the next train out of here back home to London." My mind was made up. Whether it was nonsense or not, I didn't have to stay around for it. I could always contact Alison. She'd said how much she would like to live and work in the city.

"But do you want this curse to cause the murder of innocents again? To give power to evil people?" Mrs Clark eyed me seriously. "You could stop it."

In truth I'd have been happy for some other stranger to arrive in the village and help them out on the next anniversary, one hundred years from now. But the prospect of more children needlessly perishing troubled me deeply. Could I be such a coward to let them die instead of me?

"Look, I don't know if whoever wrote that stuff long ago is right or wrong," I told my neighbour, "but the eternal damnation and death threat terrifies me. I'm not keen on dying just yet."

Mrs Clark smiled that comforting smile again.

"Times have moved on since then, and so has knowledge. I cannot guarantee the future, but I can help you in your greatest need and at least save your soul if you die."

There was little to recommend her offer. This was the moment when I had to decide if I had the courage to lay down my life for others, or cut and run. Could I ever live with myself again if I turned away? It was so easy to be brave in fiction when I was writing. This was real. No simple escape in words.

I don't know how long it was as I wrestled with my inner self. I could leave. But then I couldn't. It would haunt me forever like this bloody place.

"How can you help me?" I asked at last, with heavy heart and depressed mind.

"It may be small consolation," she said, "but I admire your courage."

Her sentiment made me feel a little better.

"Follow me," Mrs Clark walked to the door and I followed along the hallway to another door. She opened it to reveal a flight of stone steps leading down to a cellar. She switched on the light and as we descended I thought I'd been transported back to a 19th century scientist's laboratory.

Shelves all around contained glass jars with a variety of different coloured liquids. A long, wooden table straddled the centre of the room. It was covered with glass distilling equipment, test tubes in racks, a brass scale with weights and a Bunsen burner.

"This is my world of magic and medicine," Mrs Clark proudly announced, glancing round the room. "The jars contain extracts of plants, herbs and spices all growing in my garden. Mixed in the correct quantities they produce incredible powers."

I was beginning to wonder if my host was a bit loony. But this woman had seen the spirit of Beatrice approaching my cottage. Perhaps I was going loony too.

"I'll need to take a small sample of your blood," she said.

Now I began to have doubts, mainly from not wanting any blood to be taken from me.

"It's okay, it won't hurt," she reassured, opening a drawer beneath the table and taking out a scalpel, white surgical gloves and cotton wool.

From another drawer below the table she took out a necklace with a silver raven pendant and placed it around her neck. Standing still for a moment she uttered some words, as if in prayer, that I couldn't understand.

She turned and asked me to roll up my left shirt sleeve. She took my hand and with the scalpel made a small incision in my forearm. I felt no pain. Blood came trickling out and she scooped some of it into a test tube. Then she handed me cotton wool dampened with antiseptic to clean the wound.

She then repeated the blood letting process on her own arm, mixing hers with mine in the test tube.

Crossing to a shelf she took a jar with some blue liquid and added some of it to our bloods, proceeding to heat the mixture over the flame of the Bunsen burner until the contents turned a murky brown.

She poured the liquid into a beaker adding some yellow liquid from another jar until it was half full. I was again wondering what I was letting myself in for. This village was the weirdest experience of my life. The woman seemed to be into some very strange ways.

"It's all right. I know what you're thinking," Mrs Clark read my thoughts yet again. "But believe me, this will help to protect you."

Stirring the solution, now a bizarre, glowing yellowy-brown, she raised the beaker to her mouth and drank half the contents. Then she handed it to me.

"Drink the rest," she said.

I hesitated. It looked repulsive.

"If you want my protection, you must drink it," she insisted.

Reluctantly I put the beaker to my lips. The liquid contained our blood, let alone what else she'd put in it. But the potion hadn't appeared to harm her, so I drank the solution. Amazingly it tasted wonderful, like a mixture of summer fruit juices.

Mrs Clark smiled.

"Now our spirits are united," she said.

We left the cellar and she led me to the front door.

"Remember. If you find yourself in danger, in the moment of your greatest need call my white witch name – Lucinda."

I thanked her, not entirely convinced the ceremony we'd been through was any more than just pagan nonsense. But the woman was sincere and meant well.

As I started to walk away, husband Bill reappeared from their garden.

"I thought you'd gone back to your cottage," he said.

"No. Your wife has been very kind. I told her all about the strange things that have been happening to me and she has given me her protection." I assumed he knew she was a white witch and specialised in spiritual matters.

"Ah, she's been here has she?" he replied. "She was here last night and told me about the broken branch on your tree."

I was puzzled. He seemed to be referring to his wife as an occasional visitor.

"I keep the garden as she liked it. The herbs, spices and flowers. She comes sometimes to do some gardening in her own way."

"But I was with her in the cellar just now. Didn't you see her when I came here with you?" I began to feel my blood run cold.

"Yes, the cellar. She called it her cavern. Amazing things she did there. I've looked after it since she died. Wanted to keep it as her special preserve." Bill spoke in a nostalgic tone.

"Since she died....?" I began to feel dizzy.

"Yes. Five years ago. But we still keep each other company."

Now I was totally freaked out. I'd been talking to her ghost. She'd touched me. Mixed our blood. She couldn't be dead. Bill was playing a bad joke.

"But I've just come from the cellar. She took my blood. Look here's the cut..." I pulled up my shirt sleeve. The skin on my forearm was smooth. Not a mark on it.

Bill smiled kindly at me.

"There are things we cannot understand on this side. Believe me. If my late wife gave you her protection then you can be sure she will be with you." Bill placed his hand on my shoulder reassuringly.

I looked at him doubtfully.

"Wait here," he said.

He went into his cottage and returned shortly with a newspaper, showing me his wife's obituary dated March 1958.

I struggled to take it in.

"If I can help you in this world, don't hesitate to ask," Bill said, closing the newspaper.

I'm not sure if I thanked him, my mind was too confused to know what I was doing for a while. I was seriously growing worried about my sanity. I'd keep my promise to Alison and go to the Burning Beatrice festival, but after that I'd get the next train home. Whatever was going down, I wasn't going with it.

CHAPTER 10

I RETURNED to the cottage in a dazed state, hardly able to come to terms with the fact I'd had physical contact with a ghost. Or had I?

Checking my arm again it was unblemished. No wound. I must have imagined it. This was deeply worrying. Alcohol in times of pressure was not my thing, but I poured myself a generous glass of wine in the hope of settling my nerves. The whole village appeared to be something out of the 18th century come alive with a modern twist.

I went upstairs to the bedroom and pulled out my suitcase from under the bed to begin packing my clothes for an early departure first thing in the morning. I'd nearly emptied the wardrobe and was placing a shirt into the suitcase when a cold feeling came over me. The sense of a presence behind. I resisted turning to look, but once again curiosity overcame me.

My God! The ghosts of the children were standing there, only feet away, looking as solid as flesh. The boy in ragged clothes, the girl in a threadbare, dark green dress.

"Don't leave us now," the girl pleaded tearfully.

The boy took hold of his sister's hand to comfort her.

"You're the only one who can save us from wandering lost forever," he echoed his sister's misery.

"Save you? How?" I heard myself asking, as if the apparitions standing there were actually real.

"You must cut..." the boy began.

We were interrupted by a loud knocking on the front door. The ghosts disappeared.

For a moment I stared at the empty space where they'd stood. My heart racing again. The knocking intensified.

"I must cut..." the boy's words repeated in my head. What must I cut?

I couldn't ignore the door knocking any longer.

"All right. Wait a bloody minute!" I shouted. Pressure. Too much pressure. I was near breaking point.

Descending the stairs and opening the front door, I was greeted by a smiling postman dressed in a dark uniform and peak hat.

"Sign for delivery," he said, holding out a parcel. It was a surprise as I wasn't expecting a delivery. I took the package and scribbled my signature on the clipboard form.

Was it from my mother?

I opened the parcel on the kitchen table and stared at the contents in horror.

Two cloth dolls were stitched together at the waist. One a naked man. The other a woman in a long dress wearing a black pointed hat like a witch. A depiction of them fucking.

My horror turned to fury. I picked up the effigy and flung it at the wall. It bounced off and flopped to the floor.

What sick mind had sent me this?

The image of Rupert and Josh sprang to mind. I snatched at the brown wrapping paper on the table to see where it had been posted. I suspected locally, but the ink on the postal frank was too smudged to read.

Were those two into some sort of voodoo? Rupert knew a lot about the dark arts. I had no doubt the naked doll was meant to be me having sex with the hag.

But how could I prove who sent it? Sergeant Fellows was hardly going to launch a major investigation even if he could, which was unlikely. It was unpleasant, horrible, but not exactly life threatening. It was bloody scary though, and my nerves were already frayed. This was gradual psychological destruction.

I loved Alison, but we needed to get out of this place. In a few hours I was due to see her at the clothes shop. I'd issue an ultimatum for her to come to London with me or else we must say goodbye. I was that close to the edge.

Now I wondered what ghouls and apparitions were waiting in the cottage to haunt me everytime I turned around. Would they forever haunt me?

Picking up the doll effigy from the floor, I threw it into the bin as a symbol of contempt for whoever sent me the package.

I went back upstairs to continue packing, dreading the appearance of yet another unwelcome spirit. Every creak of a floorboard, rattle of breeze on the window, the odd crack of the cottage's timber frame. All stabbed at my nerves.

I couldn't spend another night here. Perhaps I could ask Alison to persuade her mother to let me stay at their house for my last night. If not, I'd rather sleep in the open and call a taxi to take me to the station in the morning.

Finishing my packing, I left the suitcase in the bedroom to collect later. Now was the time to meet Alison at her shop as planned. Usually there were people still milling around, but as I entered the high street everywhere looked deserted. Everyone was probably at home preparing for the festival.

It was in my mind to call on Rupert, but his shop was closed, and I wasn't sure where a confrontation with him might lead me. He'd probably deny sending the doll effigy and even if he admitted it, where would that take me? A weird thing to do, but not illegal.

Alison's shop was closed when I arrived. I rang the doorbell. No reply. I rang it again. Still no answer. She was probably in the back room. I rapped on the front window. No answer. Maybe she'd forgotten our arrangement. Or perhaps she'd decided to ditch me and go to the festival with someone else. My heart sank. I couldn't leave it like this. I'd go to her house.

The thought of her rejecting me and giving her affection to someone else would drive me totally insane.

I walked the short distance to the narrow street of white, terraced houses where she lived, praying all my fears were unfounded. That she'd just forgotten our date at the shop.

I was about to knock on the front door when it opened. Alison's mother stood there glaring at me.

"What are you doing here?" she barked sharply.

It threw me for a second.

"I....I was wondering if Alison is in," my voice stuttered.

"No she isn't!" came the venomous reply. "There's been nothing but trouble since you came here. Why don't you just sod off back to London where you came from," Emma's dislike of me spilled out.

"I'd planned to meet Alison at her shop, but she isn't there," I explained, ignoring the abuse.

"I've just got back from staying with a friend. I'm busy unpacking. Alison isn't here. She's probably with her friends, so just clear off. We don't want you here." Emma slammed the door shut.

Maybe Alison was with friends, or maybe she was at home and didn't want to see me. Whichever, it was clear my presence was no longer welcome.

I thought about Barbara's party invite after the festival. The last thing I felt like right now was partying. But perhaps Alison would be there. Maybe I could persuade her to come to London with me if I could just see her.

As I walked away from the house, men and women dressed in witch and wizard outfits were beginning to leave their homes, filling the streets in gowns of black, green, purple, red, emblazoned with zodiac symbols, crescents and stars. A swarm of pointed hats bobbed along the route as the townsfolk gathered and headed towards a field at the back of the town for the Burning Beatrice bonfire.

It was almost dark and torchlights shone the way with excited chatter and laughter filling the air. I felt out of place in jeans and denim jacket, but found myself swept up in the movement of the crowd heading to the witch burning ceremony.

The atmosphere was strange, as if I'd joined a group of villagers belonging to a past dark age, lost in pagan magic and spells where mob rule decided your fate. If you were an outsider who brought ill fortune they'd turn on you. I felt like that outsider, and if this crowd wanted to be my accusers, I'd stand no chance. We weren't so far away from the past.

My instinct was to leave, but I wanted to see Alison. I couldn't make out anyone familiar, especially with everyone covered in robes lit only in streaks of torchlight as we neared the field.

Stewards in hooded gowns guided us into a circle around the high pile of wooden crates and old furniture that would be Beatrice's pyre. Torchlights focussed on her effigy, shackled to a stake emerging through the top of the heap. The crowd yelled as the beams played over the sunken eye sockets and hooked nose of her moulded face.

"Burn the witch!" the cries rang out. It felt strange, as if we were being transported back in time to the real burning of a human life. Events took an even creepier turn when from the darkness, four hooded figures emerged holding blazing torches, the flames licking greedily at the night.

If I'd wanted to leave, I couldn't now, hemmed in by a crowd that was becoming more excited by the spectacle.

"Burn her! Burn her!" Yet more cries rang out.

One of the robed figures stepped forward addressing the spectators.

"Good citizens," he shouted. "We are here to celebrate the burning of that evil witch Beatrice on this day two hundred years ago. The day when our wise and brave ancestors sent her packing into the flames of hell!"

Cheers rose all around.

"Burn her! Burn her!" Now everyone joined in the chorus. The mob wanted Beatrice's destruction. Nothing else would satisfy.

The robed men turned to the stack and held out their torches to ignite the pyre. The wood was obviously steeped in accelerant as the flames burst into life, leaping savagely towards their target Beatrice at the top.

Loud cheering broke out. Children excitedly tugged at their parents arms. 'Look mummy the witch is burning'.

The flames grew larger, glowing ashes sparking off into the night. Soon they leapt at Beatrice's effigy. The hem of her robe caught fire. She tilted on the towering stake, the hooked nose of her mask vivid for a few seconds in the glare. Then a cascade of flames violently flared, devouring her as she collapsed and disappeared into the heart of the fiery inferno.

The cheers were deafening. The witch was gone. But as her image descended into the bonfire, I swear for a moment in the swirl of flames,

I could see the face of the hag who'd haunted me at the cottage. Her effigy was destroyed, but she was still coming for me.

A few seconds later fireworks began rocketing into the sky. Explosions of colour, shrieks of joy and deafening booms. Now the crowd was transfixed in hypnotic delight.

Next moment I felt jostling beside me and saw a figure struggling to approach through the throng.

"Found you," came a familiar voice. It was Barbara. She wore a pointed hat, her face lit by the glow of the bonfire. She was a comforting sight among strangers.

Reaching me, she kissed my cheek and looked at my clothes.

"Where's your costume?"

"Alison's shop was closed and she wasn't at home," I explained.

"Well, she must be somewhere here. I expect she'll be at the party."

"I'm not sure I want to go to the party," I told Barbara. Much as I wanted to see Alison, my sense of alienation in this village increased my desire just to go home. These weren't my people.

Barbara was disappointed.

"You must come. You're our special guest. I've got friends who want to meet an author from the big city," she insisted.

"I'm not exactly an author yet," I played down her comment, but felt flattered with the credit.

"You know where my cottage is. I'll be really cross with you if you don't come." Barbara held me by the shoulders and kissed me sensuously on the lips. The woman knew how to manipulate me. I wanted to reach under her robe and have her on the spot. She pulled away smiling.

"Naughty boy," she laughed. "Come to the party. London isn't the only swinging place." Her comment made me wonder what type of party was being planned.

I agreed to go, but was determined not to be drawn into a sex orgy. I hoped Alison wasn't into that sort of thing, and I couldn't believe Malcolm would tolerate Barbara engaging in it. Though she did have a powerful influence over him. Over me too for that matter.

"See you later." Barbara smiled again and disappeared back into the crowd.

After fifteen minutes or so the firework display came to an end. The crush of witches and wizards began to dissolve as they made their way toward the lights of a funfair further across the field. Music broke out as yet more festivities came to life.

In the glow of the bonfire embers, I saw a man in a police uniform approaching. It was Sergeant Fellows.

"Mr Roberts," he called, drawing close to me and talking in a whisper.

"Two young children have gone missing. I don't want to cause panic, but I need to raise a search party. If everyone here knows, it'll just be a disorganised rabble causing confusion."

His words struck horror. Was some bastard going to sacrifice two more innocent lives in a murderous black magic ceremony?

"What do you want me to do? Which children? What do they look like?"

""Quiet!" The sergeant raised his hand for me to keep my voice down. "We need this to be organised. I want a team. I have a lead."

He paused before whispering again.

"I want you to go to Barbara Carpenter's cottage and tell her. There are people going to her party who we can organise into a team," the sergeant issued his order. "I'll be there shortly. I'm just going to the police phone box down the road to let my superior know."

I didn't hesitate. Barbara's cottage was on the edge of the village about half-a-mile away, at the end of a narrow lane. I ran all the way and hammered loudly on the front door. Barbara opened it.

"You've come!" she embraced me. "I didn't know you were so keen. You nearly broke down the door."

"Two children have gone missing. Sergeant Fellows is coming. He wants to form a search party," I gasped breathlessly.

"Steady, steady," Barbara placed her hand on my shoulder. "Come inside. Have a drink. Tell me what's happened."

She led me through to the kitchen and poured me a glass of wine from a jug on the table.

"Drink this and calm down."

I took a generous swig and told her what the sergeant had said to me.

"It's the 200th anniversary of Beatrice's burning. I'm really worried that Rupert and Josh are behind it. God knows what atrocity they're planning," I was nearing panic.

Barbara looked concerned.

"Well we can only wait and see what the sergeant has planned," she decided. "Follow me and try to relax a bit."

I followed. Barbara had changed clothes since the bonfire. She now wore a black blouse, her arms covered in teasing see-through lace, and a very short mini-skirt revealing every inch of her thighs. Delicious flashes of her black panties could be seen with the slightest bend of her body.

I pushed sexual thoughts away. Two children could be in danger of their lives.

Barbara led me down the hallway and opened a door. A flight of steps led down into a surprisingly large cellar, oak beams spanning the ceiling.

The scent of incense filled the air and the room was lit by shell-shaped uplights on the walls. Shelves and a display cabinet were filled with what looked like symbolic ornaments. Ornate gold and silver bowls and chalices. Egyptian and Anubis ritual figurines, corn dollies, a variety of small cauldrons and a Wicca crescent shaped boline knife.

A wall to one side had a broomstick attached to it, surrounded by carved wooden masks glaring evil, grotesque expressions. Long red drapes covered the other walls. An uneasy feeling of danger was surfacing.

Inside a large inglenook fireplace a log fire blazed. In front of it a high-backed wooden chair, like a throne, was positioned facing into the room. Beside the chair stood a low table with a gold bowl resting on it. Lighted black candles formed a semi-circle around the setting.

Then to my total horror I saw it. A portrait of the witch who'd haunted me at the cottage. Beatrice cruelly stared at me from above the fireplace, her image framed in ornate gold surround. Two red candles burned at each end of the mantelpiece and cast a flickering light that seemed to animate her terrifying features.

"What the hell! Is this some bad party joke?" I turned on Barbara. She just smiled.

"Welcome home. You have found your destiny."

I was confused.

"Take your seat. You are going to help us rise to the heights of this very special night."

Barbara beckoned me towards the chair. Now I noticed she was wearing a necklace with a large, silver pentagram resting on the fold of her breasts.

I felt unsteady. The room blurred for a moment. I found it difficult to concentrate. Barbara took my hand and led me through a gap in the candle semi-circle to the chair. I didn't want to go there, but I was having difficulty in resisting. My own will seemed to be drifting away. Somewhere in the growing dullness of my brain it occurred that Barbara must have drugged my wine. Everything was clouding into a dreamy haze.

"The children! We must help find the missing children." The urgency of saving two young lives from danger struggled to surface in my wavering mind.

"We already have them," Barbara stood before me continuing to smile a smile that was now taking on depths of evil.

"You have them?" I couldn't understand. Surely she wasn't going to slaughter them in some ritual?

"They're here," she announced. As she spoke another figure entered the room. Malcolm, her fiancée was dressed in a trailing, black robe with a scarlet stripe down the front. He held an object in his hand. My focus was drifting in and out, but after a few moments I could see they were bones. The ones I had seen at Rupert's shop. The murdered children's thigh bones.

But they'd been confiscated by Sergeant Fellows.

"We don't need to slaughter any children. These bones are much more powerful. They have powerful spiritual qualities from the last invocation of Beatrice, when the children were murdered and sacrificed one hundred years ago."

Barbara stood in front of the chair staring down at me, her eyes dilated and penetrating. Malcolm approached and placed the bones each side of the gold bowl on the table. Barbara picked up the bowl.

"Malcolm has ground a little from each bone and mixed it. See here." I looked into the receptacle and saw a small pile of grey dust. She placed the bowl back on the table.

"The other magic ingredient to summon the powers of Beatrice is human blood mixed with the bone dust." She paused and stared at me.

"Your blood."

Her smile was now cold. I realised to my horror a diabolical death was planned for me. My instinct was to escape. But try as I did my limbs had now become incapable of movement. The drug in the wine was paralysing.

Next moment another black robed figure with a scarlet stripe down the front entered the room. For a second I didn't recognise the face. Then it hit me. Sergeant Fellows! I'd mostly seen him in police uniform. Now he seemed an entirely different person.

I caught a flash of light from something he was gripping. A sword. The missing sword! Barbara must have stolen it from her mother's attic. It was all a pretence that Fellows was looking for it. I began to realise what a fool I'd been. The missing children line had been a ruse to make sure I came here.

The sword had been used one hundred years ago to cut the children's throats. Now it was going to be used to cut mine. Once again I struggled to escape, but my body wouldn't obey.

Fellows approached. Was he going to slit my throat? The drug hadn't dulled my mental terror. He laid the weapon on the table beside the bowl and bones then looked at me.

"Sorry," he said, "but it's easier to dispose of a stranger without too many questions asked than it is a villager." His apology for my impending murder was of little comfort.

"Are you all mad?" I cried. The three just looked at me pityingly.

"After your sacrifice, Beatrice will rise to give us immense powers," Barbara sounded inspired. "We will be able to bend people's wills to our own. Accumulate wealth and position at the highest level."

"And I'm not here to spend the rest of my life as a Sergeant Plod in this backwater village," Fellows interrupted. "Always overlooked for promotion by idiots." Bitterness poured from his soul.

"But you're going to murder me. Are you all insane?"

Barbara now gazed at me venomously.

"No. We are not insane. I've studied the black arts and the spells of Beatrice for years. Watch this."

She glanced upwards to the portrait of the witch over the mantelpiece.

"Sweet Beatrice. Mother of the dark earth. Send me a sign that you are near." Then Barbara removed her pentagram necklace and held it towards the portrait above the mantelpiece. A blue spark flew out circling the room and struck the pentagram. A glow of brilliant light surrounded Barbara for a moment, then broke into another blue streak striking my chest.

I screamed as unbearable pain shot through every part of my body, causing me to shake uncontrollably.

"Now do you believe me?" Barbara sneered, placing the necklace back over her head.

"I thought we were good friends," I pleaded as the pain subsided. "Why do you want to harm me?"

Barbara looked at me pityingly.

"You are a plaything. A toy. You mean nothing to me." She paused.

"I told Malcolm and Bob here about our sex. It really excited them while we were having a threesome together." She smiled at the men and they smiled back gratifyingly.

"And now before the ceremony, I'm going to excite them again as well as satisfying the desires of Beatrice, who wants you so much."

Barbara bent forward and kissed me on the lips. A soft intimate kiss. God, she was desirable, even as I feared for my life. I tried to pull away, but was still unable to move.

"Where's Alison? Is she part of your plan? Am I a toy, a plaything to her?"

"Oh, the lovers," she sneered again. "It's only because she's my sister that she's spared. She's so bloody good. Innocent." Barbara's contempt for her sister surprised me.

"Always the family favourite. I'm so glad I fucked you. That you weren't exclusive to her." The vitriol of the woman poured out. I'd never have guessed she was so bitter.

"If you want to know," Malcolm spoke for the first time, "Alison's safely detained in the attic. I put her there the other day," he grinned.

What had they done to her? I seriously wanted to fight back, but whatever I'd been drugged with, its power over my limbs remained solid.

Barbara's tone softened again.

"Don't worry. It will soon be over for you. But first Beatrice wants you through me."

She bent forward and undid the front of my jeans, pulling them down with my underwear. Now I felt entirely defenceless and ashamed as the two men leered at the spectacle. Barbara stroked my cock and I couldn't resist as my erection grew.

Then she lifted her short skirt and pulled down her black knickers. The sight sent a surge of excitement through me. I wanted to resist, but my base instincts were in control. She unbuttoned her blouse, taunting me with her beautiful full breasts.

Then she straddled me. I kissed her breasts as she guided my penis into her soft, embracing vagina. She rode me slowly at first, arching her head back as her pleasure grew from small sighs into gasps and frenzied cries at the pinnacle of climax.

I could hardly move, but it didn't dull my own growing ascent to orgasm. We shook as the intensity coursed through us. My eyes were closed in ecstasy. Slowly I opened them. I can never forget the horror that awaited.

Barbara's head was gone. In its place, the blackened, flame-scarred face of Beatrice leered at me!

"I said you would be mine," she sneered, in evil gratification, easing herself off me. Barbara's shapely body remained intact below the witch's wizened features. It was a terrifying, bizarre sight and the thought of sexual union with this ungodly creature sickened me to the soul.

"Soon, with your blood, my face will be restored to the beauty it held when I was a young woman," the witch told me.

Then she turned to Malcolm and Fellows, who also looked terrified, completely unprepared for the transformation staring at them.

"Where's Barbara?" Malcolm cried.

"She is no more," the spectre laughed. "I possess her now."

Malcolm looked angry, distressed, but backed away under the venomous gaze of the witch.

"If you do my bidding, I may return her to you," she said. The hag turned back to the table beside me and lifted the sword.

She approached, raising my chin with her hand.

"Come here," she ordered Malcolm. "Hold the bowl with the children's bone dust under his throat."

Malcolm stepped forward and obeyed.

Now my heart pounded furiously, my body straining to escape, but still my limbs refused to budge.

The witch raised the sword to slit my throat.

"Let him go!" a shout echoed across the room. Standing by the cellar entrance, woodkeeper Josh was aiming a shotgun. Rupert carried a cylinder on his back and pointed a hose attached to it.

Beatrice lowered the blade and stared contemptuously at the intruders.

For a second I felt relief and amazement. The two I believed to be evil conspirators were now my rescuers.

"If you try to harm him, I'll spray you with Angelica acid," Rupert warned the spectre.

Beatrice appeared concerned for a moment.

"You can't destroy me. The recipe for the potion is long lost," she scorned his threat.

Rupert moved his arm and next second liquid shot from the hose he held, spraying the witch. She recoiled in pain, staggering briefly. When she recovered, she looked defeated.

"As you wish. I shall release him," she agreed, slowly replacing the sword on the table.

Then swiftly she grasped the pentagram resting between her breasts and held it up. Two blue streaks of light shot from it, striking Rupert and Josh. The force threw them backwards, sending their bodies sprawling across the floor with enormous impact. They lay still.

Unconscious or dead. I didn't know which, but my only hope of surviving this horrific night had now been lost.

Beatrice lifted the sword again, commanding Malcolm to hold the bowl with the children's bone dust under my chin again.

I shook with dread, but my limbs remained unable to move. The razor sharp edge of the weapon hovered only inches from my neck. I began praying for help as Beatrice drew back the blade for the cut. She was laughing, relishing my fate. Where would I go when I was dead? A vision of my parents and sister flashed before me. I'd never see them again.

Then the ghost appeared in my eyes. My next door neighbour.

"Call my name in the greatest danger," her words echoed.

"Lucinda!" I cried out.

A brilliant bolt of light struck Beatrice's arm. She staggered around in pain as flames seared along it. Screaming she dropped the sword, beating her arm to put out the fire.

My body suddenly felt as if it was loosening up. I shifted my legs, my arms. They moved and I swiftly hitched up my jeans.

Malcolm had backed away, confused and looking fearful. Fellows was retreating to leave the room. The sword lay on the floor.

I leapt for it grabbing the handle. Beatrice was recovering, She saw my move. Quickly, she reached for the pentagram round her neck. I had a fraction of a second. If a streak from it hit me, I'd be lost.

Rushing at her I swung the sword blade with all my might.

It struck her neck, but didn't stop, slicing through flesh and bone. Her head flew off, hitting the floor with a heavy thud. It rolled for a moment before coming to a stop. Blood jetted out from the remains of her neck, spraying everywhere. The body which had once belonged to Barbara lolled around for a few seconds, then collapsed on the floor.

For what seemed an eternity all was still, save for the crackling log fire. I was in a state of shock. The hag was destroyed, but I'd also executed Barbara.

Malcolm stared in horror at the seperated head and body on the floor. His face turned scarlet with fury.

"You vile bastard. You've killed Barbara!"

He rushed at me. In defence, I swung the sword towards him, pointing the blood-soaked blade to ward him away. But the momentum of his attack was unstoppable. He ran straight into the tip, rapidly jerking to a halt as the blade entered his stomach and sliced through his body exiting his back.

Blood cascaded from the wound in a torrent, spraying my face and clothes. I recoiled and spat as some of the liquid entered my mouth. The weapon slipped from my grasp as Malcolm tottered backwards. He briefly looked down at the handle protruding from his stomach, stunned amazement on his face. Then he collapsed.

Now Fellows approached.

"You're finished," he said. "I will be a witness that I came here undercover, and caught you in a black magic ceremony murdering Barbara and Malcolm."

He was a police officer. His word would count over mine no matter how much I protested the truth.

I looked over at Rupert and Josh. They lay lifeless on the floor. The candles that had been arranged in a semi-circle around the chair were now scattered on their sides, knocked over in the struggles. Their flames extinguished too.

"You'll hang for this," Fellows snarled my fate grimly.

"How will you explain the witch's head on Barbara?" I replied, trying to play for time. To find holes in any explanation he might offer to a court.

"What witch's head?" he asked.

I glanced to where Beatrice's head had rolled. It had transformed in death back into Barbara's head and was staring vacantly upwards. I'd escaped from one horror to another. There was no proof of her transformation into Beatrice. Not only was my defence lost, but Alison would hate me forever for killing her sister.

As Alison came into my mind, I remembered Malcolm telling me she was safely detained in the attic. Imprisoned more likely. What had they planned for her? However much she would hate me, I had to find and release her.

I started moving towards the cellar steps. Fellows stood blocking my exit. I heard a groan. Rupert was stirring on the floor. Slowly he sat up, dazed but still alive. Fellows seemed agitated. Josh began to revive.

"There are my witnesses," I shouted at Sergeant Fellows. He leapt at me. I managed to dodge aside. Then he rushed across to Malcolm's lifeless body and with a heave withdrew the sword sheathed in his stomach.

Raising the blood red weapon, Fellows ran wildly at me, slashing the sword like a madman. I jumped back, raising my arms instinctively in defence. The blade sliced across my forearm. I yelled in pain as blood oozed from the wound. Fellows was in for the kill. I had no protection. My eye caught sight of the chair I'd been imprisoned on.

I grabbed the back and swung it upwards. Fellows struck again. The blade chopped into a leg of the chair. I backed away, using it to fend off the vicious blows, trying to edge myself towards the cellar exit and escape. Pieces of the chair were breaking away with each strike. As I moved around, Fellows neared the burning log fire. The hem at the back of his robe brushed across the flames.

My defence was almost gone as the chair disintegrated. Now only the back of it remained. Fellows raised the blade and with all his force swung it down. The chair back split in two. My protection was lost. He raised the blade again, grinning triumphantly for the death blow. Then he froze for a second and screamed in pain.

Flames were engulfing his back, rapidly spreading round his robe. It must have caught alight when the hem brushed the fire. He dropped the sword in panic and tore off the garment, throwing the burning remains away. For a second he seemed confused, standing there in scorched underwear.

Then swiftly he stooped to pick up the sword. As he bent down, I kicked his head hard. He staggered and fell on the floor, blood trickling from his temple.

"Quick! Get out!" a cry came from Rupert, who was moving awkwardly as if his limbs were unable to function normally. Josh was resting on one knee, struggling to raise himself.

"The place is going up," Rupert shouted.

I'd been totally unaware of the surroundings, but could now see the red drapes around the room beginning to flare. The burning robe Fellows had thrown off had landed and ignited one of them.

The flames were now shooting across the drapes like wildfire. We couldn't possibly put them out at the rate the fire was spreading. Choking smoke started filling the room.

"Get out now!" Rupert repeated, helping to lift Josh to his feet.

The blaze began flaring along the wooden ceiling beams as the varnish on them melted, accelerating the flames and spewing out dark, toxic fumes.

The room was fogging, becoming difficult to see and breathe. Out of the swirling smoke a figure suddenly lunged at me, fists homing-in for attack. A deafening blast shook the room. There was just enough visibility to make out Josh pointing a shotgun. My attacker staggered back and collapsed.

"That bastard sergeant won't trouble us again," Josh growled. Fellows lay still on the floor.

"Alison's in the attic," I cried out. "I've got to save her."

The three of us started towards the cellar steps, Rupert and Josh still finding it hard to move easily.

"We'll call the fire brigade," Rupert said. "They can use ladders. If you try to rescue her alone it'll be suicidal. The place is going up fast."

I couldn't wait for the fire brigade. It would be too late. I sprinted out of the cellar and up the stairway to the landing.

The hatch door to the attic was too high up in the ceiling for my arms to reach. And it was locked by a sliding bolt secured by a padlock. Loud thumping broke out from above. Alison was definitely in there. She must have heard the noise from below.

"I'm coming for you," I shouted to her. But how in God's name would I reach the hatch door and get past the padlock?

Smoke was beginning to billow up the stairway.

I saw a half-open door and rushed in. It was the bedroom. There was a chair facing a dresser. I could reach the hatch door with it, but I'd need something solid to smash the bolt away. Frantically looking round I could only see ornaments, toiletries, clothing on the bed. I threw open a wardrobe, shoes, boots and more clothes. Useless to smash the bolt. My heart sank and then I saw a hand dumbbell laying in a corner.

Grabbing the metal weight and chair I returned and started smashing at the bolt, breaking it away from the hatch door.

Pushing back the lid, I could see no ladder inside to pull down, so I gripped the hatch edge and hoisted myself up. It was pitch dark beyond the light entering from the landing. There was a muffled cry for help. As my eyes adjusted a little to the darkness I could make out a figure seated several feet away on a chair, gagged and arms bound behind. Rushing across, I pulled off the gag.

"Get me out of here!" Alison screamed, struggling to free her arms. They were secured to the chair back with thick, plastic cord.

It was too tight to pull away, and with nothing to cut it I couldn't release her short of dragging the chair to the opening and pushing her through, at the risk of causing injury or death. I said I'd be back and hoisted myself out of the attic to find something sharp.

"Don't leave me here!" Alison yelled in panic.

Smoke was now thickening into a fog, swirling across the landing. Shafts of heat punched me as I ran back into the bedroom. I could see nothing to cut the cord. I opened another door on the landing. It was stacked with shelves of books. Astrological charts and pagan symbols adorned the walls. Beside one chart a sickle with an ivory handle was fixed to the wall.

I grabbed the handle and wrenched away the implement. The sickle's razor sharp edge would easily slice through the cord. As I re-entered the landing, flames leapt at the bottom of the stairwell.

Throwing the sickle through the hatch opening, I clambered back up and swiftly freed Alison from the binding. Her limbs were stiff from imprisonment and I guided her to the opening. She was shaking, traumatised.

Her distress escalated as she stared down through the hatch at the landing below.

"You'll just have to grab hold of the sides and lower yourself," I urged. She hesitated, but seeing no other way knelt down, grabbed the sides and dropped on to the chair below. Quickly I followed.

To my horror, the fire was now consuming the staircase, smoke thick and choking, The heat was unbearable. Loud cracking filled the air as the cottage timbers began to give way. We entered the bedroom and I opened the window. Now our only chance of escape would be to jump out. It looked like a fifteen foot drop to the ground. Enough to break limbs on impact or even end up dead. Remaining, however, gave no chance of survival.

Alison looked as terrified as I felt, but I had to pretend all would be well to calm her. She'd obviously been through hell trapped in the attic and now this. There was no sign of the fire brigade arriving. In this remote village things moved slowly.

I'd closed the bedroom door against the flames. Suddenly it exploded inwards, pieces flying across the room in a searing blast of fire. The floor beside it collapsed and more flames burst upwards into the gaping opening. The cottage was collapsing.

"Now! We've got to jump now!" I shouted.

Alison was in panic. I slapped her face.

"Do it!" I yelled. She was frozen in terror.

I lifted her on to the window sill. Then shoved her out.

The floor beside me collapsed. Scorching flames shot through burning my back.

I leapt up and jumped out the window.

Terrible pain shot through my right leg as I hit the ground and rolled away from the building. The only good fortune was that the landing was on a garden lawn and not solid stone. But Alison was uppermost in my mind. I looked around, then saw her wandering in confusion. She'd survived, thank God.

The last I remembered was the side of the house where we'd been just moments before. A blast of heat struck me as it erupted into a gigantic inferno.

****

I WOKE up laying on a hospital bed. Rupert sat on a chair beside me.

"Welcome back," he smiled. "I'll fetch the nurse."

After being thoroughly checked over I was given a clean bill of health save for the swollen sprained ankle sustained when I jumped out of the cottage window. The horrifying events of the previous night began surfacing in my head.

"You'd better come and stay with me," said Rupert. "The nurse says you shouldn't be alone for a while just in case you have problems."

I limped down the corridor as he walked beside me to the hospital exit.

"Never mind me. Where's Alison?" I asked. Her welfare was my main concern.

"She's at home. It's alright, she's safe," Rupert assured me.

"I want to see her."

"I don't think you do. Not at the moment," he replied in a tone of warning.

I started to feel unsteady. Faint. I'd chopped off her sister's head. Well not *her* head, the witch's. But it was Barbara's body. Rupert grabbed my arm to steady me.

"She thinks I killed her sister?"

"I don't know. You're a stranger. There are rumours going around you started the fire."

"Me?" I was shocked. "But I saved Alison." I couldn't believe what I was hearing.

"You know I didn't start the fire. It was Fellows."

"Yes, but in a small village people believe what they want to believe. And strangers are always the main suspects."

Now I was stunned.

"The police will want to interview you, along with me and Josh," said Rupert. "We came back after calling the fire brigade and found you unconscious on the lawn. The police arrived and said we'd be wanted for questioning."

It was only as we left the hospital that I realised it was early evening. I'd obviously been out cold since the previous night.

He drove me to the cottage to collect my belongings. I wasn't sorry to be leaving the place. Then we went on to his flat above the bookshop.

On the way Rupert told me Barbara and Malcolm's cottage was entirely destroyed by the fire. Both of them and Fellows would have been charred beyond recognition. It was a terrible thought, even though the three had been intending to kill me for their own evil ambitions. Death by fire seemed to be the hallmark of the Beatrice curse.

At Rupert's flat we sat in armchairs with a good brew of tea and I began to relax a little. The room looked as I'd imagine the home of a bookseller. Shelves stacked with books. Magazines in scattered piles around the floor and a record player on a side table with a collection of classical records in a rack beside it. Posters of bookcovers adorned the walls.

We talked and I explained to him what had happened after he and Josh had been rendered unconscious by Beatrice. How I'd been forced to sever the witch's head from Barbara's body. And I told him how the white witch Lucinda, or Mrs Clark, had come to my rescue.

"I knew that Mrs Clark had died, but I never knew she was a white witch," Rupert was amazed by the revelation and her rise from the dead.

"You must have some special attraction to the supernatural," he concluded.

If I did, it was not an attraction I relished.

We were silent for a moment before Rupert spoke again.

"I'm sorry I doubted you."

His remark puzzled me.

"I thought you'd been drawn into Barbara's web and become part of her diabolical plan," he explained.

"And I thought you and Josh were hatching some diabolical evil for the Beatrice festival," I admitted. "But why did you suspect Barbara and her fiancée? She never gave the slightest indication of any interest in the occult."

"It was through a friend who runs a bookshop in a town twenty miles from here. Through a casual conversation he mentioned that a woman called Barbara frequently visited his shop and was very interested in legends about the witch Beatrice."

Rupert took a sip of his tea.

"I don't know why, but something made me wonder if it might be Barbara Carpenter from our village. And if so, why would she travel twenty miles to another bookshop when the same information about Beatrice could be found near her home in my shop?"

Rupert placed the cup and saucer back on the small table beside him.

"I asked my friend if he could find out her surname. And when she wrote a cheque for a collection of his books on the occult, he saw it was Barbara's surname. Carpenter." Rupert sat back in the armchair, clasping his hands in thought.

"He also told me she'd asked him if there was a shop that sold occult charms. Her obvious interest in the supernatural became evident, especially linked to Beatrice. Yet no-one in the village had any idea she was interested in spells and charms. It made me suspicious."

Rupert picked up the teapot and offered me a refill. I declined.

"Then one night Josh was patrolling the wood and saw a torchlight and two figures digging around in the spot where you and I found the skeletons of the murdered children. When they left he followed them, and in better light saw it was Barbara and Malcolm. He told me about it and I could only imagine they could be searching for some remnant of the children. A part of their bones that might have been missed after the remains had been removed."

It began to dawn on me where Rupert was leading.

"The couple had left empty-handed. I'd read in one of the legends that bone of the murdered children could be used in black magic as a substitute to harness Beatrice's power, instead of the need for another murder. The only pieces of bone unaccounted for were the thigh bones, which, stupidly I realise now, I'd kept as a historic memento. When Sergeant Fellows confiscated them I was angry, but thought at least they'd be secure from any evil misuse."

Rupert lowered his head in regret.

"I never realised Fellows was part of their plot too, and would give the bones to Barbara."

On that we shared equal blame. I wouldn't have told Fellows about the bones if I'd known he was part of the plot.

Rupert resumed his story.

"Josh and I decided to close in on Barbara and Malcolm. We searched for the missing sword at the old chapel, because we knew it had to be used in the ceremony, but we couldn't find it."

"That's because it was really kept in the attic at Alison's home. Barbara stole it," I told him.

Rupert paused for a moment as another part of the puzzle fell into place for him.

"Well, as you know, Josh helped me prepare an attack on them at their cottage on festival night. Seeing you as the victim though was a total shock to us."

Our conversation was suddenly disturbed by the urgent ringing of the doorbell and loud banging on the shop window downstairs.

"Hold on. I think I know who this is," Rupert looked grim. He hurried downstairs, returning shortly followed by two police officers.

"We'd like both of you to come with us," said one. It wasn't a request we could refuse. The police car took us to the local cop shop. We entered the building to see Josh already there.

He stared at me with those glowering eyes making me feel I'd done something terrible. Then he approached me. I stepped back, thinking he was about to launch an attack. Next moment he held out his right hand, gripping mine in a crushing handshake.

"I never knew you had it in you. Well done! You showed amazing courage," he growled.

For a second I thought I detected a glint of admiration in his eyes. He released my hand and the sullen face returned.

A door opened. Another sullen face appeared in the shape of a heavily built, middle-aged man in a grey suit, his hair slicked back as if to hide encroaching baldness.

"Mark Roberts?" He looked at the three of us standing together. I nodded.

"I'm Detective Inspector, John Shepherd. Come with me."

I followed him down a dull green corridor into a battleship grey interview room.

"Sit down," he beckoned as he sat on a chair opposite me at the table.

"Now tell me what happened at Barbara Carpenter's cottage from the moment you arrived. And I'll know if your lying," he added coldly.

His manner was unsettling, but I had no intention of telling him anything other than the truth. I explained what took place. Then I got to the bit about Barbara mounting me on the chair and her head turning into Beatrice's.

Now either he'd laugh cynically at me or say I was lying, but he remained totally unmoved. The only bit that seemed to register a reaction in his eyes for a moment was when I described my fight with Sergeant Fellows, and Josh blasting the officer with a shotgun.

I knew death by hanging was the punishment for killing a police officer, and as an accomplice in the attack I could swing too. But if I lied now, any plea of self-defence would look shaky should I change my story later.

When I finished, I fully expected to be arrested and charged with murder. The detective wrote something on the notepad and stood up.

"Right. You can go. But don't leave the village. You may be needed for further questioning." He turned and I followed him out of the interview room. The outcome was far better than I'd expected, but the prospect of being hanged was still on the cards while the investigation continued.

As I re-entered reception, Rupert and Josh were waiting there. They'd been interviewed separately and were equally surprised at not being arrested and detained.

Josh came back with us in the police car to Rupert's flat. His normal ice cold manner had thawed a little and he offered to make us a meal. His familiarity with the flat and knowledge of where everything was situated led me to think of him as a regular visitor. Even to consider the possibility that he and Rupert were more than just friends.

I didn't feel hungry. My appetite was dulled by worry. Josh prepared a delicious lasagne and I ate some of it, apologising for not being able to finish the meal.

We talked of the dreadful events at Barbara's cottage and what we'd told the police. All of it was the truth from our own perspective and we knew that death by hanging could be our fate. Short of fleeing and going into hiding, which would make us look guilty, all we could do was wait and hope for the best. That our story was believed.

Beheading a woman who I thought had turned into a witch didn't appear convincing as a defence, except perhaps to have me declared insane and condemn me for the rest of my life to an asylum. I'd be alive, but it would hardly be worth living.

Josh left shortly after and Rupert made up a bed for me in the spare room.

It wasn't a restful sleep. My dreams took me back to the awful events in the cottage and several times I woke in a heavy sweat. The thought of being hanged also became more vivid as the distractions of daytime were stripped away. I could see myself standing before a judge pronouncing the death sentence on me. Eventually further sleep was a frightening prospect.

I got out of bed and went into the living room. The light was on. The wall clock pointed to just after 5.30 in the morning. Then I saw Rupert sitting in an armchair.

"You couldn't sleep too?" he sympathised. "Let's have a cup of tea."

He stood up and went into the kitchen. I sat in the other armchair and he returned a few minutes later carrying two mugs.

"I've got to see Alison," I said.

"I'm not sure that's a good idea," he replied.

"I love her."

"I don't think the feeling will be mutual," he advised frankly.

"As far as she's concerned, you killed Barbara. The locals are saying you started the fire. And if she learns you cut off her sister's head..." he paused. "Sorry to put it so bluntly."

"It wasn't her sister," I protested. "It was...." Then I realised the only witnesses to the event were the three of us facing murder charges.

"I don't care. I've got to see her. To try and explain. They kidnapped Alison. I saved her life."

"Don't do it," Rupert warned.

The thought of never seeing Alison again tore me apart.

"I'm going to see her. At the very least to say sorry for what I had to do. I must."

Rupert shook his head.

****

NEXT day I set off for Alison's house. It would not be easy trying to justify my actions in killing her sister.

As I approached the house, the feeling grew of eyes behind lace curtains following my every move down the street. It was unnerving. I knocked on Alison's door. A few moments later it opened. Her mother, Emma, stared at me in hate.

"Murderer! You killed my daughter with the sword, then set fire to her cottage!" she screamed. God knows how she knew what had happened at the cottage. Someone from the police must have leaked it and now the story was probably skewed beyond truth.

"Let me explain."

Emma didn't want my story. She spat in my face.

"I saved Alison!" I pleaded in vain.

Next moment she struck me in the chest with her clenched fist. I staggered back. She advanced to attack again.

Doors along the street were opening. Neighbours piling out.

"Fuck off! Get out of our village," voices shouted.

"String the bastard up!"

Now I feared for my life. It looked like a lynch mob was starting to gather. I turned and ran as hands reached out to stop me. I dodged them making for a gap in a closing swarm of people, just managing to escape through it. I'd never run so fast. A group pursued me as I sped down side streets without knowing where they led.

After what seemed an eternity I saw the wood ahead and ran into it. Seeing a cluster of trees and bushes I headed for it and hid behind. Footsteps tramped across the undergrowth.

"He went that way," someone called.

"No that way," another voice countered.

The voices grew nearer. I laid down flat, my heart racing furiously as I tried to control my gasping breath. The group looked around for some sign of me, then turned and moved off.

"We'll get him," came the determined threat from a man, as my pursuers made their way back out of the wood.

Now my only thought was to escape from the village. I'd be more likely to swing here long before any judge could pronounce sentence in a court. But all my money and belongings were back at Rupert's shop.

I remained hidden in the wood for hours. Only when the sun began to set did I venture to leave. I had a rough idea of the direction to the high street and as darkness fell I quickly made my way back to the bookshop.

Rupert was sweeping the shop floor when I arrived outside and tapped on the window.

"You were right. It was a bad idea," I said as he opened the door. "A lynch mob came after me. I'd better leave now. I don't want to put you at risk for helping me."

"There are no connecting trains to London tonight," said Rupert, ushering me inside. "And I'm not throwing you out to the wolves."

For someone who I'd suspected of being evil, his kindness touched me. How could I have been so wrong about him?

"We'll get you safely out tomorrow," he assured me.

Rupert made a meal in the kitchen as we discussed how he would take me to the station in the morning out of sight in the back of his van. He'd buy the ticket and then I could slip out as the train pulled in, spending the least time being visible.

I had another restless night.

It was early morning when I heard the loud smash of breaking glass. At first I thought I was having another bad dream. Then I heard Rupert moving outside on the landing. I leapt out of bed. Confused. Sensing danger.

Rupert was halfway down the stairs as I came out and followed. The shop's display window was shattered. A brick rested among the fragments of glass and books scattered across the floor. Rupert stepped carefully over the pieces and peered through the opening. The high street was deserted. Whoever had thrown the brick had disappeared.

For a moment we stood there shocked and puzzled. Rupert in his dressing gown and me in my underpants.

"I've got some plywood boards in the garden shed," he said, and left through a side door. I went upstairs to put on some clothes.

Rupert returned with the board, a hammer and some nails.

"Someone obviously knows you're staying here. Word will spread. We've got to get you out as quickly as possible first thing." He began hammering the board to cover the opening.

I'd have to leave most of my possessions here. A large case would just slow my escape.

It was still dark outside at six as we prepared to leave for the station so I could catch the early connecting train home.

The doorbell rang, followed by loud tapping on the glass door pane. We looked at each other wondering what new danger lurked. Rupert carefully lifted a slat on the blind covering the door and peered out.

"It's a police officer," he whispered. "Maybe he's come to arrest us."

Oddly, I felt relief at the possibility. At that moment it was preferable to being savaged to death by a wild mob.

Rupert unlocked the door.

The officer was studying the plywood boards.

"Did you sell someone a book they didn't like?" he commented dryly. On another occasion we might have enjoyed his joke.

"I was driving by and saw the boarding. Wondered if you'd had some trouble?" he was now taking his role as a police officer seriously.

I was sure I'd seen him somewhere before, and after a few moments remembered it was the policeman who'd been at the desk when I'd visited the police station to see Fellows. The one who the sergeant had described as ambitious and full of illusions about going places.

Rupert invited the officer inside and explained what had happened. Now he did look serious.

"Well, you're not exactly the most popular man in town." He glanced at me. "But we won't have mob law."

The officer saw my travel bag on the floor.

"All packed up and ready to go I see."

I explained my need to get away. That Rupert was going to tell the police where I'd gone.

"That would be silly. Only make it worse for yourself," he shook his head.

"I'm desperate. I don't want to be strung up in a mad frenzy," I protested.

"Calm down and just listen to me for a minute," he said, raising his hand to quieten me.

"I was going to call you into the station later this morning, but now is as good a time as any to tell you. Can we have a chat in more comfortable surroundings? And a cup of tea would be welcome."

Rupert invited him upstairs and we settled down in the living room. My nerves were on edge wondering if he was trying to deliver bad news in a friendly way. He was not what I expected a policeman to be and seemed to waver between being serious and lighthearted. I wondered, as he sat on the armchair sipping his tea, whether he was deliberately holding us in suspense for fun or some sort of unpleasant satisfaction.

"This is a really nice brew," he said, complimenting Rupert on the tea.

"Just tell us!" I could stand the tension no longer.

"Oh sorry," he said. "Yes. You're free to go."

The room seemed distant for a moment. I found it difficult to take in his words. Was the stress so great I was now imagining a happy outcome?

"There are no charges against you," he continued.

The look of relief in Rupert's eyes was palpable.

"Why?" he asked.

"I shouldn't really tell you. It's confidential."

I was content to leave the matter there. We were free and I couldn't wait to get away to avoid confrontation with an angry crowd.

"But personally I feel you're owed an explanation. Though I would deny it if you ever said I'd told you." The officer placed his tea cup on the side table beside him.

We assured him we wouldn't say a word except to Josh. The policeman accepted our promise, settling back in the armchair.

"I spoke to a senior officer some weeks ago about a strange conversation I'd had with Sergeant Fellows," he began. "But my superior dismissed what I told him as nonsense. Then after the fire at Barbara's cottage, a team of investigators went to Fellows' home."

The officer paused. He was obviously finding it hard to relate the story.

"In a locked desk the investigators found a diary that Fellows kept. In it they saw references to his contact with some people in the village, and how he was planning with them to sacrifice a life on Beatrice bonfire night to raise the witch and be rewarded with supernatural powers. The names of the others involved were not recorded in the diary."

I looked across at Rupert as the revelation unfolded.

"There was no mention of the intended victim, but he wrote that some bones of the murdered children could be used in the invocation ceremony. That he'd discovered them in Rupert's bookshop."

It appalled me that I'd been the one to direct Fellows to the bones in my total ignorance.

"He also mentioned about 'the sword being safe'. Of course the diary changed the whole nature of the investigation."

He stopped to take another sip of tea.

"But what was the strange conversation you had with Sergeant Fellows some weeks before?" I was curious.

"He drew me aside one night when we were both on duty and asked if I would like to receive special powers. I thought for a moment he was talking about a promotion. Then he went on about joining a group who could invoke supernatural powers. A ceremony on the 200th anniversary of Beatrice's burning at the stake."

The officer shook his head remembering the conversation.

"I thought he was mad. I laughed and dismissed black magic ceremonies as complete nonsense. I wish now I'd gone along with it. Could have saved a lot of grief if I'd got undercover information on them all." He frowned regretfully.

"Of course, Fellows became nasty to me after I rejected his offer. Spread word that I was an incompetent fool. Only after the tragedy did my superiors take me seriously."

Rupert and I said nothing for a moment, thinking about the officer's lost opportunity to prevent the catastrophe.

"So we're free to go because the police force doesn't want to tarnish its reputation. A sergeant involved in a black magic ceremony with intent to murder." Rupert came straight to the point.

"Exactly," confirmed the officer, without a hint of trying to gloss over the motive.

"Both you and your friend, Josh, will be publicly exonerated. A story will be given to the media that a fire broke out at Barbara and Malcolm's cottage while they were preparing for a party, and Fellows along with yourselves tried to rescue them. Unfortunately, Sergeant Fellows perished in the blaze. You'll be heroes."

I wasn't sure this village would ever hail me as a hero, and I still wanted to get away as soon as possible. The story would be a lie, but I don't suppose the truth would please anyone either.

Looking up at the wall clock, I saw it was quarter to seven. I'd miss my train if I didn't leave quickly. The officer stood up.

"You're worried about a wild mob attacking you." He read my thoughts.

"Get your travel bag and I'll take you to the station. Your train leaves in half-an-hour."

His offer was music to my ears. A safe passage out of here. I said a hasty goodbye to Rupert and we agreed to meet again one day.

On the way to the station, the officer told me he'd been successful in applying for a job with the Metropolitan Police in London.

"So I'll be in your neck of the woods soon, the Smoke," he said. "I'm Police Constable, Alan Anderson. And one day, hopefully, I'll be a detective superintendent. So keep out of trouble, or I might have to run you in." As he drove, he turned to smile wryly at me for a second.

I couldn't make him out. Never quite sure if he was being serious or taking the piss. Fellows had been right though. Constable Alan Anderson was certainly ambitious. I wondered if our paths would ever cross again.

I thanked him as he dropped me off round the corner from the train station, so the police car wouldn't draw attention. I stepped out of the vehicle. He called back to me.

"And don't forget. If you or your friends ever breathe a word of what I've told you, you'll all end up on a murder charge - and be hanged." On that, he was definitely being serious. I felt a bristle of fear and nodded that I understood the terms of our pledge. The relief was overwhelming as I closed the car door and walked towards my freedom.

There were a few people on the station platform and I prayed they wouldn't recognise me. Fortunately I passed unnoticed, keeping my head slightly lowered.

As the train pulled into the station my eyes wandered to three figures further along the platform. I nearly dropped my travel bag in shock. The spirit woman Lucinda, who'd saved my life at the black magic ceremony, stood there with the two murdered children. They smiled at me and were gone. I remained in a trance for several moments wondering if I'd actually seen them, or if it was just my imagination.

On the train my thoughts turned to Beatrice. Her curse was unforgivable. But she had also been a victim of lies and false accusations, which likely led her to become demented as her flesh fried and sizzled in the dreadful death of burning at the stake.

For her curse she deserved to be in hell. Then so too her accusers, who probably continued to live on happily without a blemish on their names.

But what clouded my thoughts was the prospect of never seeing Alison again. And knowing that she would hate me for the rest of her life. That was unbearable.

****

SIX months after I returned to London, my father suffered a sudden heart attack and died. I immediately had to take over the running of the family business. My intended career as an author was put on hold.

Another five years passed before I decided to revisit Deersmoor village. In all that time I was haunted by the thought of wanting to see Alison again. To apologise for what I had done and explain why I'd needed to kill her sister. Though I could never expect her forgiveness.

This time I drove to the village in my blue Ford Anglia, so I could make a quick getaway if the villagers were still after my blood.

I also chose to arrive as evening was falling, to avoid prying eyes recognising me easily. I'd since grown a moustache and my hair was cut shorter, giving me a slightly different appearance.

It was strange driving down Deersmoor high street. The place was largely the same throw back in time, but Rupert's bookshop had gone. I pulled up outside for a moment. The premises had been converted in a newsagent shop. I could only assume Rupert's business had finally gone broke. It was a great shame. He was a good man and deserved better. Driving on, I parked the car round the corner from Alison's house.

Of course, the whole mission was pot luck. Rupert had gone. Alison could well have left the village too. The other possible terror awaiting was the prospect of her mother, Emma, answering the door and rallying the whole village against me. A good reason why I came by car so I could make a quick escape if necessary.

I knocked on Alison's door. No reply. I knocked again. Still no reply. Now I began to dread someone coming out of another house and recognising me. Since there was obviously no-one at home, I decided to return to the car and perhaps try again another time.

I started walking back and turned the corner nearly colliding with someone approaching. I apologised. Then saw who it was. Alison!

She didn't recognise me for a second. The moustache must have confused her. We stood staring at each other, a thousand thoughts of the past shuffling through our minds. Our meeting, our love, our terrifying parting.

"How are you?" I heard the words tumble from my lips and they seemed ludicrously inadequate, as if we were just casual friends who hadn't seen each other for a while.

I expected her to spit at me. Hit me. Scream in anger.

She just continued to stand there, staring. Not saying a word. I felt on trial.

At last she spoke.

"Have you come to write another book?"

I couldn't be sure if she was being sarcastic or making a genuine enquiry.

"No...." I faltered. "I've come to apologise for the dreadful sorrow I caused you and your mother."

Her eyes were penetrating.

"You put my life through hell. You put my mother's life through hell."

I shrank in guilt.

"But my sister, Barbara, also put your life through hell."

She understood. I couldn't believe it. She understood.

"Rupert and Josh told me all about it. And that policeman, Andrews...."

"Anderson," I said.

"Yes. Anderson confirmed the story. For the horror she caused you, I'm sorry."

Another silence fell between us.

She looked as beautiful as ever. Dressed not in the mini-skirt style I remembered, but in a blue shift dress with white cuffs and collar.

"I've never stopped loving you," I said. I had to let her know my feelings, even if it was the last time we ever met.

"Well, since you're here, you'd better come into the house."

Her reply was not what I expected. None of it was like I'd expected.

"But if your mother comes....?"

"My mother is dead. She died two years ago."

"I'm so sorry."

"No you're not. Don't lie. Come on."

I walked with her to the house. It reminded me of the first time we'd met and I'd accompanied her to visit her dying grandmother. The beginning of it all.

We entered the kitchen. It had been refitted with Formica counters since I was last there. The old cooking range was gone.

Alison opened a bottle of wine and we sat at the kitchen table.

"I don't think I could ever entirely forgive you for killing my sister." Her words struck me hard. I could hardly expect her forgiveness.

"But I wish I'd listened to you more when you were telling me about Beatrice and the strange events." She poured wine into our glasses.

"For a few months before it all took off, my sister had started behaving oddly," Alison explained.

"When I visited her, I noticed she'd begun to lock the cellar door. In the past we'd gone down there to listen to records. But suddenly it became out of bounds. She said it was being redecorated, so I left it at that. It didn't seem a big deal."

Alison took a drink of wine.

"I also saw a couple of books in the living room about ancient charms and ceremonial pagan rituals. Barbara wasn't normally interested in things like that. I took it they belonged to Malcolm. And when the sword went missing, something flashed through my mind that Barbara might have something to do with it."

She took another sip of wine.

"But I didn't want to believe she could be involved in black magic. Barbara was always a down to earth person and dismissed supernatural stuff."

She paused.

"How wrong could I be? If I'd listened to you, it might have forced me to put two and two together, and I could have confronted her."

"And possibly put your life in greater danger," I said. I could never tell Alison of the vitriolic jealousy Barbara had hissed about her sister on that horrific night.

"Is that cursed sword still around?" I asked.

"They told me it must have melted in the fire. I don't know for sure. I hope so. And I pray that vile witch Beatrice will never be able to rise again."

The vibrant Alison I had known now looked burdened with sadness and regret.

"Do you still want to come to London?" I plucked up the courage to ask.

"I've carried on working at the clothes shop. I haven't felt like doing anything new for years. Don't go out much either."

I wanted to hold and comfort her, but the time wasn't right. Not just now. She was carrying a lot of unpredictable hurt.

"If you ever wanted to come to London, I'd help you to find a place to live. Even help you find a job," I offered. "But I'd understand if you never wanted to see me again. I just wanted to say I'm sorry, and let you know that I care."

Alison didn't reply. This was the final goodbye. At least I'd been able to apologise.

"One day," she said.

"One day?"

"One day I might go to London."

I couldn't work out if she meant taking up my offer to help, or if she wanted to go in her own right.

"If you do, call me. Here's my number." I took out a business card. It seemed a bit formal, but it was all I had to hand.

"Company director," she read from it.

"My father died. Writing has taken a back seat."

"Life has changed a lot for us," Alison reflected.

"I'd better get on my way," I stood up feeling it was time to leave. Alison came to the front door.

"I see Rupert's bookshop has gone," I remarked. It seemed a trivial comment while my heart was slowly breaking apart.

"He moved to another part of the country with Josh, a few months after you left," Alison explained.

"I had an idea they were more than just friends."

She nodded, confirming my thoughts.

As I stood in the hallway by the open door, I looked at Alison for the last time. I couldn't stop myself from leaning forward to kiss her. She didn't draw back as my lips lightly touched her cheek.

"Goodbye." I turned and left, tears streaming from my eyes as I returned to the car.

****

LIFE moved on after my sad parting at Deersmoor, and I met and married a wonderful woman.

Nearly fifty years have passed since then. In all those decades I only recently finished writing the story of that extraordinary episode in my life.

Sitting on the sofa beside my wife one evening, I handed her the manuscript of those amazing events. Alison took hold of it and flipped through the pages.

Yes. If a miracle never comes to me again, I'm grateful for the one that did.

A year after our parting, I was sitting in the office at work when my sales manager came in saying a woman was asking to see me. I could hardly believe my eyes as Alison entered the room.

"I've finally made the break and come to London," she said.

"I will try my best to forgive you, if you will try your best to forgive me for the hell my sister put you through," she offered the compromise. I would forgive her anything.

This time nothing was going to hold me back. I took her in my arms and we kissed, no more barriers between us.

Not long after she set up a successful clothes boutique, thriving in the fashion explosion of the 1960s and 70s. Our son and daughter arrived too, now adults with their own children.

As we sat together on the sofa, Alison finished flipping through the manuscript, not really reading it, then handed it back to me.

"You said the police officer warned you never to say a word about it, or the case might be re-opened," she reminded me.

"I can't believe any of them would be bothered by now. It was a long time ago. And I think the public should know, just in case Beatrice ever rises again."

After all these years, I still wondered if the witch had truly been vanquished.

Mention of the episode brought back painful memories for Alison. Time to let it rest for the moment.

I placed the manuscript on the floor, then sat back on the sofa putting my arm around her shoulders.

"Well, maybe our son or daughter will publish it one day. Or the grandchildren. Until then, it will remain our secret."

MORE BOOKS BY THE AUTHOR

I hope you enjoyed THE BEATRICE CURSE. If you would like to read more of my books they are listed below and available through Amazon.

As a taster, here's the first part of my popular novel:

THE SOUL SCREAMS MURDER

THE FIRST two weeks in their new home were the happiest times for Paul Hunter and his family. After that, events descended into a nightmare.

Paul was an architect and had slogged dutifully as an employee of a large corporate for 16 years since qualifying in his mid twenties.

The move was part of his plan to set up as a freelance architect, and gradually build a business in his own right.

Of course, he had no idea of what awaited.

His wife, Diane, was an experienced public relations consultant. She too had worked for a large organisation, and also had plans to form a business.

But first she would spend time re-organising the house to suit the style the couple desired, including structural alterations. And, more importantly, help their daughters, Alice 11 and Rosemary 14, settle into their new surroundings and the local school.

The house was a big, four-bedroomed property with a large garden beside a quiet, leafy lane in the village of Lynthorne. A considerable step-up from the small, three-bed semi where they had lived, forty miles away, in a traffic-clogged suburb of outer London.

The sisters had been reluctant to move at first, leaving behind friends, but soon adapted well, enjoying the benefits of beautiful, open countryside on their doorstep.

The first two weeks of happiness, however, came to an abrupt end one night, when the girls were sharing a bedroom while re-decoration took place.

Rosemary, the older sister, had not been able to sleep well that night. She was having strange dreams in which bizarre figures were trying to steal something precious from her. She awoke, feeling uneasy. In the dimness of a night light on the chest of drawers, she saw an elderly man and woman standing at the foot of the bed, staring at her.

For a moment she was frozen in terror. Then she calmed down, thinking perhaps the couple had lost their way and wandered into the house by mistake.

"Are you lost?" she asked. They continued to stare at her, looking troubled as if they were seeing some portent of ill fortune.

Rosemary's voice woke her sister Alice, sleeping in the bed beside. She looked up and, seeing the couple, screamed.

Paul and Diane shot bolt upright in bed, awoken by the piercing sound. In seconds they had crossed the bedroom, and were speeding down the landing to their daughters' room. Alice was crying, terrified by what she'd seen.

"There were ghosts in our room," she insisted as her parents attempted to comfort her.

"You've had a bad dream, that's all," Diane reassured her.

"But it was an old man and woman. They were staring at us," Alice would not be placated.

Paul turned to Rosemary.

"Tell Alice it was a dream," he felt sure confirmation from her sister would calm the girl.

But Rosemary was looking pale. She remained silent for a moment.

"I saw them too," she replied, quietly. "And now they're not here."

Paul and Diane searched round the room and then the house, wondering if an elderly couple had found their way into the property. But no-one else was present. All the entry doors and windows were locked.

For the remainder of the night the girls slept with their mother, and Paul stayed in the girls' bedroom. As daylight broke, no further disturbance had occurred.

Both girls still looked shaken as they sat half-heartedly eating their breakfast. Diane was concerned and suggested they stay off school for the day. But their desire was to get out of the house for a while.

"I'm sure you didn't actually see ghosts," their mother tried to reassure them as she made a coffee. "Sometimes dim lighting can make things in a room look like something else for a moment."

Her daughters looked unconvinced.

"We both saw them!" they replied.

"Then they were gone. They disappeared into thin air," added Alice. "This place is haunted."

Diane didn't reply. Youngsters had vivid imaginations. She could offer no rational explanation for what they believed they had seen. But she was certain it was nothing supernatural.

"I'm not sleeping in that room again," Alice insisted, as she rose from the kitchen table to collect her school bag.

"Nor am I," Rosemary agreed, joining her sister.

"Well, daddy and I will move into your room and you can both sleep in ours," Diane offered a solution. The girls settled with the offer.

As Diane was leaving to drive them both to school, Paul appeared at the top of the stairs. He'd been on the phone in his makeshift office, talking to a new client.

"Have a good day girls," he called to them, "and don't worry. There's no such thing as ghosts."

His daughters said nothing, and left the house with their mother.

On Diane's return, Paul came down from his office to have coffee and chat with her in the living room. They sat on the sofa amid a setting of chairs, tables, dressers and lamps, which still hadn't found their rightful place in the house while re-decoration was continuing.

"I'm worried about the girls," Diane voiced her thoughts.

"It's a new home for them. Youngsters imagine all sorts of things," Paul sat forward on the sofa, clasping the coffee mug in his hands to warm them."

"But they couldn't both have seen these..." Diane hesitated to find the right word, "...people."

"One of them thinks they see something and describes it to the other. Next moment they have both 'seen' or imagined it too," her husband gave his explanation of the strange visitors in the girls' bedroom. "Kids just have over-active imaginations. I did. Can't believe you didn't too."

His wife didn't disagree, but still appeared doubtful.

Paul place his mug on the coffee table beside him.

"You're not telling me that you actually believe in ghosts?" he asked, incredulously turning to face her.

Diane sipped her coffee, looking thoughtful.

"Well...no," she paused. She was an educated woman. Belief in supernatural beings seemed primitive, something that was understandable as a belief in earlier times, but didn't fit with the sophisticated, modern world.

"No, I don't believe in ghosts," she hesitated.

"But perhaps something dreadful happened to someone here. Perhaps they leave some sort of energy behind, something that manifests itself in a way we don't yet understand. That someday science will be able to explain."

Diane wasn't sure if she'd convinced herself with the explanation, let alone her husband.

He stared at her, shaking his head in disbelief.

"Well, in all the years we've been married, I never thought you believed in spirits and all that hokum."

"I don't," she protested. "You misunderstand."

"What dreadful thing do you think has happened here?" Paul asked.

"I don't know." His wife looked confused.

They decided to leave it at that, and discuss instead how they could best help the children restore the happiness they'd enjoyed in their new home until the previous night.

For the next few nights all was peaceful, the manifestation seemed to have ceased. Then the couple were awoken by a piercing scream in the early hours, coming from the bedroom they'd swapped with the girls.

They ran to see what was wrong and found their daughters hugging each other, looking terrified.

"What's happened?" Their parents were fraught.

"We saw them again!" Rosemary struggled to speak, shaking.

"They were standing by the bed, looking down at us as if they were trying to tell us something."

"All right, it's all right. We won't leave you alone at night again," Diane cuddled them.

"We'll find out what's going on. Ghosts don't really exist. Perhaps something or someone is playing a nasty trick," their mother tried to offer a rational explanation.

"What did they look like?" their father wondered if a description might be valuable to the police. It was possible intruders may have somehow gained entry.

The girls were too confused to offer any useful description, except Rosemary had noted the man had a large, red birthmark on his left cheek.

Diane slept in the room with them for the rest of the night.

Next day, Paul left the house to see a client. Diane took the children to school then returned home, wondering how she could get to the bottom of the strange appearances the girls had seen.

She made a coffee in the kitchen. Her thoughts also touched on the spare bedroom upstairs where she had plans to set up an office and start her own public relations business. She needed to keep focussed on that as well.

Paul had lost a sizeable income leaving his company to branch out and build a business of his own. In the meantime, she would need to help boost their funds.

Diane left the kitchen, carrying her coffee, to make her way upstairs and look over the bedroom which would be her future office. She was still deciding where the desk and equipment would be best placed. She hadn't made a final decision.

At the bottom of the staircase she looked up. Standing on the landing she saw an elderly man and woman gazing down at her.

She leapt back in fear, dropping the coffee mug, which shattered spreading the contents across the tiled hallway. When she looked up again, no-one was there.

Diane rang her husband and told him what had happened.

"I'm in the middle of an important meeting. I can't discuss it now," he sounded impatient. "This business has made you all start to imagine things. I'll get back as soon as I can." He hung up.

Diane was beginning to think he was right, but she was reluctant to go upstairs on her own. She felt silly. A grown woman afraid of...imaginings. But if it was imagination, it held a powerful grip. After spending time reasoning that it may well have been just her imagination she went upstairs, cautiously, fearful that any second the old couple might appear. All the rooms were empty. But the emptiness echoed a sense of foreboding.

The next couple of nights once again passed peacefully. Paul, for the reassurance of his family, now slept on his own in a single bed, while Diane stayed in the other bedroom with the girls. It was becoming ridiculous, he thought. He really must find out who was causing this charade so normal life could be restored.

He was becoming convinced there was a secret entry into the house and some neighbours, for whatever reason, were playing unacceptable pranks. Ghosts did not exist. Of that he was absolutely certain.

When yet another night passed without disturbance, Paul began to think the drama was over.

His hope was short lived.

At breakfast, Alice was eating her cereal with her sister and parents at the kitchen table.

"Why were you arguing last night?" she suddenly posed the question to her mother and father.

They looked at each other quizzically.

"We weren't arguing last night," Diane replied.

"I heard you," the child insisted. "I woke up in the middle of the night and you weren't in the bedroom," she looked at her mother. "You were downstairs arguing with daddy."

Diane and Paul were totally baffled. They'd both gone to bed at the same time and hadn't left the room all night. Certainly they hadn't been arguing.

"You were saying something like 'he'll be the finish of us all,'" Alice looked at her father.

"And you said 'just leave him alone,'" the girl turned to her mother.

"Who were you talking about?"

"I think you must have been dreaming, darling," Diane had absolutely no idea what her daughter was talking about, but like her husband, was beginning to wonder if the house was starting to cause their daughters psychological problems.

Alice's older sister, Rosemary, was not aware of anyone arguing in the night, but her feeling of unease was plain to see.

Diane took the children to school and returned to the house. Her husband was out again meeting a client.

Her original feeling of happiness in the new home had dissolved and was now replaced with apprehension. She feared seeing the appearance of the old couple again and kept looking behind, wondering if they were standing there, watching her.

She told herself to get a grip. It would be intolerable to continually live in a state of fear. Spirits did not exist her rational self insisted. But deep in her primeval psyche, dread of the unknown ruled.

She walked into the kitchen to make a coffee when the doorbell rang. It was the postman delivering a parcel. She'd ordered a necklace and opened the package in the hallway, examining the jewellery, then trying it on to see if she liked it in the reflection of the hall mirror.

Satisfied with the purchase, she returned to the kitchen to make the coffee. Her eyes caught sight of a carving knife laying on the counter beside the knife-block. Her mouth dropped in horror. She hadn't removed it from the block. Of that she was certain. Or was she?

Perhaps she had, absent-mindedly. But she would have remembered. Or perhaps someone or something else had removed it. The knife wasn't on the counter when she'd left the kitchen to answer the postman's call. A chill ran through her. Was it those...?

Diane wondered if she should ring her husband. It would sound pathetic. A grown woman letting her fear run away with her. But the children were suffering. This house was not good. She rang Paul and told him about the knife. As expected, he wasn't sympathetic.

"You obviously put it there without remembering. You're always putting things somewhere then forgetting where you've put them. This business is getting out of hand." His frustration at the disruption of family life was getting to him.

"Just try and relax. I'll talk to you when I get home this evening."

"I'm not spending another night in this house," Diane decided to put her foot down.

"The children are suffering and I won't let it go on. I'm taking them to stay with my parents for a while."

Paul was silent for a moment.

"Look, can we talk about this when I get back? It shouldn't be too late."

Diane agreed, but she didn't plan to hang around for long.

When her husband returned, he saw two suitcases in the hallway. Diane and the children were wearing their coats, waiting to leave. Paul became angry, slamming his briefcase down on the floor.

"You can't just leave like this," he shouted. "What about their education?" He pointed toward the children.

"They don't want to stay here. They're not going to learn much frightened out of their wits," Diane replied. "I'll find another school."

Paul's anger melted into sorrow.

"We had such plans. What about them?"

"We'll have to work something out," Diane offered a compromise.

"These apparitions, they're just imagination. Can't you see that?" Paul pleaded.

"That may be. But they're very real to us. We're not staying here." Diane was unmoved.

"We'll sell the house. Find somewhere else," Paul bargained. "Will that make you happy. Will you stay until then?"

Diane agreed with selling the house, but adamant she and children would live with her parents in the meantime.

"But their house is sixty miles away in Bridgeworth. I can't work here and visit you every day. It will have to be weekends." Paul was deeply upset at the prospect of being parted in this way.

Diane and the girls were also extremely sad to be separated from their father. But relieved at not spending another night in the house.

Paul hadn't experienced the strange activities his family had encountered. It was difficult for him to understand a problem which, for him, did not exist other than in their minds. He kissed them, and with a heavy heart, watched them leave.

That night he decided to sleep in the main bedroom, where he'd originally slept with his wife before his daughters' nightmares had started. Nightmares. Unreal phantoms. That was his simple explanation for their unfounded fears.

He felt very lonely. Only a few weeks ago the house had rung with happiness. Now the silence in the absence of his family seemed to hang heavily in the air.

He climbed into bed and turned off the bedside light, laying still, wondering what he could do to make his wife and daughters feel comfortable in the house again. He was reluctant to sell so soon. Only a short time ago, it was going to be the location of a fresh, new start in life. The launch pad for him and his wife to become successful entrepreneurs in their own right.

Paul's thoughts must have been overtaken by sleep, for he opened his eyes suddenly, sensing time had passed without him realising. It came into his head he'd been awoken by a sound.

But all was silent.

Then he heard voices coming from downstairs.

The surprise sent a shot of fear through him. Were there intruders in the house? Would he have to deal with them? Was it the tricksters who'd been terrifying his family?

Silence fell again. He turned on the bedside light, and as he started to look around the room for an implement to defend or attack, he heard a man's voice crying out.

"Put the knife down, for God's sake!"

It sounded like a struggle taking place. Things smashing on the floor, chairs scraping, falling over. It was followed by a woman's piercing scream.

Paul's blood ran cold as he grabbed a pair of scissors from the dressing table and flung open the bedroom door. Someone was being attacked downstairs.

Darkness and silence confronted him through the open door. He fumbled for the landing light switch and turned it on. Cautiously he moved to the top of the landing stairway, listening, looking with hawk eyes.

It was dark and silent downstairs. The landing light cast his elongated shadow eerily down the stairwell. Paul was fighting hard to suppress his growing feeling of terror. Slowly he descended the stairs, every creak amplified, every glance magnified.

What happens next?

THE SOUL SCREAMS MURDER by Geoffrey Sleight.

Available on Amazon

More books by the author

DARK SECRETS COTTAGE

Shocking family secrets are unearthed in a haunted cottage.

A GHOST TO WATCH OVER ME

A lost letter revealed by a ghost leads to treachery and corruption at the highest level.

VENGEANCE ALWAYS DELIVERS

A stranger's friendly advice is packed with a vendetta of vengeance.

THE ANARCHY SCROLL

A dangerous mission in a mystical world of spells, spirits and sorcery

All available on Amazon

Please contact me if you have any questions or would like information about forthcoming books. All emails will remain entirely confidential.
geoffsleight@gmail.com

Visit my Amazon Author page:
http://amazon.com/author/geoffreysleight

Printed in Great Britain
by Amazon